# Ring Around Rosie

A NOVEL

by

Emily Pattullo

# Chapter 1

Rosie stood staring at the gate; her unfinished painting discarded in the long grass that rolled gently on the cliff edge. The sign said Danger. Keep Out. Private. But what could be so private around here, in the middle of nowhere?

'No!' she said to herself, turning away, her mother's voice ringing in her ears. 'I promised not to get into any more trouble.'

She picked up the painting from the ground and held it to the light. It was a shockingly bad representation of the scenery before her. How had she thought she could do it justice with her limited artistic ability? The sea looked like grey mud, and the sky something from a child's picture book, complete with token fluffy cloud (or a legless sheep).

'I can't do it!' she stormed, walking into the kitchen and slamming the painting down on the worktop. 'There's no point me even trying.'

'Of course there is, darling,' her mum soothed. 'The therapist said it would really help keep your mind occupied, stop you thinking about everything that happened in London. Don't give up, I think it's beautiful. In fact, I'm going to hang it above the fireplace,' said her mum, picking up the painting and holding it aloft. 'I think the colours will really complement the curtains.'

'Thanks, Mum, but I'd prefer it if the whole world didn't get to see my first ever painting.'

'The whole world?' scoffed her brother, Ted, walking in and opening the fridge. 'You'll be lucky if a passing sheep sees it way out here!'

'Come on, guys,' said their dad, appearing from behind his newspaper. 'I know it's secluded but apparently this stretch of cove was a popular spot with smugglers back in the day. The estate agent told me there's an actual smugglers' path up the cliff; it's really treacherous, he reckons. And he said the smugglers often lost their footing and plunged to their death on the rocks, especially when they were over-laden with treasure. Oo arrgh!'

Rosie looked over at Ted and rolled her eyes. 'So you're saying they were real pirates, then?'

'Well, no, not necessarily, I was just doing that for effect; you know, adding a bit of foreboding to the story, help you sleep tonight.'

'Great, Dad, very scary,' snorted Ted.

'Alright, Cheery Beard, don't enter into the spirit of the place, then. I think it adds to its character though, don't you, Bella?' he said, looking to his wife for support.

'Absolutely.'

'And you wouldn't have found any smugglers or pirates in London, now would you? Maybe a few drug barons but not genuine one-legged villains. There may even be a few old barrels of rum or moonshine washed up on the rocks too!'

'What's moonshine?' asked Rosie.

'It's illegally distilled spirits, like whisky. It was notoriously the drink of choice for English smugglers.'

'Now yer talking!' said Ted, with a mouthful of food. 'Where can I get this stuff?'

'Clue's in the word *illegal*, Ted,' said their mum, laying the table. 'And I'm not sure talk like that is hugely appropriate, Sam,' she scolded her husband, nodding in Rosie's direction.

'Oh please, Mum; like I'm going to race down to the beach and start licking the rocks in case there's a-hundred-year-old alcohol on them. Give me some credit!'

'Sorry, Posie, you're right. And I know you've learnt from past mistakes and are really trying to make a fresh start.'

Rosie scowled at the nickname she hated. 'Yes, I am,' she sniffed. 'And some support from my family would be good rather than always assuming I'm going to fuck up again!'

'Rosie!'

'Sorry, but how can I make a new life here, like you want, when you're always watching me, expecting me to slip up? I've said I won't drink anymore, not that there's anywhere to buy alcohol from anyway – you made sure of that – and I won't get arrested again either! I won't do anything, at all, ever!' she shouted, storming outside and down towards the cliff.

Rosie fought back the tears that stung her eyes; angry at herself for being weak and wishing she could have a drink because then at least these feelings that she didn't know what to do with would numb themselves into something manageable.

She flopped down on the cliff edge, dangling her legs over the side like she was challenging gravity to a battle of wills. What did her parents know? she raged. They had no idea about her life in London, the friends she hung with. They were a good, solid bunch: dependable. So what if they liked to drink and take drugs? All teenagers did that. But at least she could rely on them to have her back. Not like her mum and dad who just wanted her to fit in and conform. Rosie turned slowly and looked over her right shoulder at the gate with the threatening sign. Well, she wasn't like that, she decided, walking towards it and climbing over.

Flanked by a hedge on one side and a wooded area on the other, the path wound around and then over a small wooden bridge that crossed a narrow, sunken stream. The water was murky and bubbled around an obstacle blocking its flow. Rosie knew how it felt. The path steered her around another couple of bends before it gradually began to widen into more of a track.

Rosie stopped. To her left was another path that led down into a wood and towards the beach, and to her right was a strange building, half sunken into the ground. The roof was only one-storey high and there was grass growing up over it like it had been partially built into the earth. A bomb shelter or bunker perhaps, from the war. She remembered not really listening during a lesson at school about such things, and come to think of it, this was sort of like she imagined one might look. There were no windows but there were two chimney-like turrets protruding a couple of feet from the top.

Suddenly Rosie heard voices coming through the wood behind her. She threw herself into the hedge beside the bunker and put her hand over her mouth as if afraid she might let a noise escape.

'This is a good batch, I reckon,' said one of the voices.

'Yeah, and none of them have a clue. They still think they're here to find a better life,' said another.

'Well, better for someone, but not for them.' The other laughed.

Rosie peeped through a gap in the hedge. Three men were coming up the path through the trees, two wearing jeans and t-shirts, and one was dressed head to toe in an orange boiler suit. They walked towards the bunker and stopped just in front of it, within spitting distance of where Rosie was hiding.

'When are we heading out then? We're nearly out of food,' said the man who had spoken first, rubbing his large stomach. He had a moustache, slicked-back greasy hair, and very hairy arms. He was also half the height of the other two.

'We've been through this, Rusty,' replied the second man, rather irritably. There's going to be another drop-off and then we can leave.' He was the youngest-looking of the three, with blond spiky hair, and he had an accent that Rosie couldn't place.

The third man, the one in the boiler suit, seemed quieter. He shifted nervously from one foot to the other, wringing his hands together. He was the tallest of the three, very thin, and there was something not quite right about him, Rosie thought.

The young, blond man looked at him. 'I think it's time for your pills, Griff,' he said, patting him on the shoulder. They all walked around to the side of the bunker and went inside.

So, there was a reason for that sign, thought Rosie. Clearly those men are up to something. And what could be in that bunker? Someone had said a good batch. Weed perhaps? Moonshine even!

She would have to come back.

# Chapter 2

Ted was staring at the contents of the last unpacked box in his bedroom, wondering where he could hide some of the more private things he possessed, when the bedroom door burst open and spewed out something that looked a little like his younger sister but with a mouth that was opening and shutting like a demented goldfish.

Ted frowned and ordered her to close the door. If their mum heard him playing The Streets so loudly she'd make him turn them off.

'I… when I… I saw…' gasped Rosie.

'Spit it out, I can't understand what you're on about.'

'I found this gate and there was a sign on it that said Private–'

'So you went through it,' interrupted Ted, shoving the box under his bed to deal with later.

'Well yes, but…'

Rosie told Ted everything she'd seen and heard.

'Don't you think that sounds dodgy as?' she finished. 'Men hanging around in an old bunker right next to the sea. And they were talking about waiting for another drop-off. They could be drug smugglers!'

'Right, like the pirates Dad was on about,' sneered Ted.

'Maybe… I mean, well, no.'

'Then I don't know what you want me to say. You know what Mum and Dad will do if you go off and get into trouble, and I'm not getting blamed for you getting arrested again. So I guess you won't be finding out.'

'But if you come with me you can make sure I don't get into trouble,' Rosie suggested, her eyes pleading.

'No, Rosie! How is it you manage to find trouble wherever you go? Mum and Dad will freak, it's not worth the stress.'

'Oh poor Teddy is afraid of Mummy and Daddy,' sneered Rosie.

Ted could feel the familiar burning irritation at his sister's constant need to always do things she knew would get her into trouble.

He took a deep breath. 'Seriously, Rosie, I have no idea what you're expecting to find.'

'Life!' she burst out. 'Something to get my heart racing! Anything rather than a "blank canvas representative of a clean start", which is the answer to all my problems, according my therapist. Anything rather than the pitying, worried glances from Mum, terrified I'm going to go off the rails. I just want to be allowed to be myself, for once!'

Ted blinked disbelievingly at Rosie; her big blue eyes fierce with defiance. That was more than she'd ever said about the problems of the last few years.

'It's alright for you,' she continued, slumping down on his bed. 'You're a boy, you can do what you want. No one ever asks where you've been and who you were with, even when you come home wreaking of alcohol and smoke!'

'I'm three years older than you!' reminded Ted.

'Oh please, you sound just like Mum and Dad. Everyone knows girls are more mature than boys!'

'Not necessarily,' replied Ted. 'And not in your case. What about those freaky friends you had? Very mature bunch,' he sneered.

'Well, at least I make new friends, you've had the same ones since primary school!' Rosie scoffed, rummaging through a pile of photographs that were on the bed. 'Aw, I'd forgotten about these. Who knew you used to be so cute?' she said, holding up a picture of them both sitting side by side dangling their feet into a swimming pool in Spain. 'Oh and this one of that seagull stealing your ice cream!' She laughed. 'You cried for hours.'

'Give that here, I was about to bin it!'

'No way!' Rosie giggled. 'This one's coming out on your eighteenth.' And with that she shoved it in her pocket and left the room.

Ted started to follow her and then thought better of it; she would only start on at him again about finding out what those men were up to. He could get the photo off her later.

Ted collected the other pictures together, pausing at one of him and the boys at the river. It was a section of the Thames they could access via a small tunnel so they could search along the edge at low tide and find junk that had been washed up. Dillon was holding up a wheel from a shopping trolley while Midge and Plank threw stones at passing pigeons. They can't have been more than about eleven in the picture; very different to the seventeen they were now but still as good friends. Rosie was just jealous.

Ted missed his mates, and London. If it hadn't been for his sister and her issues they wouldn't have had to leave. And of course he'd been teased to death about it – Hunter wellies and Barbour jackets, shooting parties and games of skittles with the old dudes down the local. It was funny to begin with but then it just made him angry.

'Chin up, mate,' Dillon had said one night when Ted was ranting about his crap life. 'You can come back up and crash with me whenever you want.'

'Thanks, man.' Ted smiled. 'I know. It's just gonna be hard to get anywhere without a car, and I'll have to get work to pay for one, and I know nothing about farming or any other countryside jobs.'

'Mate, I'm sure there are other jobs besides farming in the countryside.' Dillon laughed. 'Although, you would look gorgeous in a milkmaid's outfit.'

Ted had lunged at Dillon, fists clenched, but couldn't help laughing with him.

A smile threatened to reshape his sullen lips as he thought about how they would all be heading down to the local pub and then to the Indian about now. Ted doubted there was much chance of any Indian restaurant delivering out here. What he wouldn't give for a bowl of poppadoms, an extra hot tikka with plain rice and a side of peshwari naan. His mouth started watering.

He instinctively reached for his phone. 'Un-bloody-believable! It's tuned itself to a sodding French network!' he growled.

Ted took his phone to the window and held it up. The sound of the waves breaking on the shore reached his ears and he cringed; passing cars with horns blaring, police sirens, domestics in the neighbouring house, those were the sounds he longed for. Just as he was about to give up on his phone and turn away, he caught a glimpse of movement on the water. Squinting into the retreating sun, he saw what looked like a boat heading slowly towards the cove. Probably just fishermen, he thought, smothering a yawn.

# Chapter 3

Rosie stepped onto the beach, triumphant at having found a way down the cliff despite brush and loose rock that could have dislodged and sent the whole lot, including her, crashing onto the cove below. Just because Ted was too afraid to disobey Mum and Dad, didn't mean she had to be. She had left the music playing in her room with the door closed, knowing they would assume she was still unpacking. She would be back well before they realised she wasn't there.

Small, undulating hills led steadily down to meet the sea where they were soon engulfed in its angry white teeth as it lunged at the shore, taking great bites out of the shingle and dragging it into the water, before spitting it back onto the beach in disgust.

Not the calmest of waters. Rosie shivered.

Dusk was closing in and it was getting hard to see as she scanned her surroundings, able to just make out the rocks that her dad had mentioned at one end that cast eerie misshapen shadows along the shoreline. As her gaze swung to the other end of the cove something caught her eye. At the base of the cliff, a bit further along from where she was standing, was something that looked like a head. She ran up the beach to take a closer look. It appeared to be some kind of shrine. There was a large ugly head carved out of wood at the centre, and then around it was a selection of random bits of old rubbish that must have been picked up from the beach: rope, plastic bottles, shells. There was also a one-eyed doll: old and dirty, not to mention creepy. Who could have left these here? wondered Rosie, looking around her. Theirs was the only house for miles around, which was why her parents had chosen to move here, so who could have…?

Just then a light on the water caught her eye. A boat was pulling silently into the bay. So that's how people get here, Rosie thought. She ducked down, afraid of being seen, and watched as four men walked down the beach towards the water's edge. It was hard to see in the waning light, but from their shapes Rosie thought she recognised the three men she'd seen earlier. She watched in silence as a dinghy was lowered from the boat and two of the men on the beach waded into the breakers to greet it as it pulled into the shore.

This is it! thought Rosie excitedly. They're going to offload the drugs now and Ted will be sorry he didn't want any part of this. But as Rosie watched the shadowy procession walk up the beach and disappear into the wood, she realised that it wasn't drugs they had taken off the boat at all, it was children.

'How can that be?' Rosie whispered to herself, watching as the dinghy took the other men back to the boat, leaving as silently as they had come.

Rosie started running along the beach, her feet crunching and sliding on the stones, eyes fixed firmly on where they'd entered the wood. She had to find out what they were doing; drugs was one thing, that was understandable, but children? It didn't make sense.

She reached the yawning mouth of the wood; it was horribly dark and creepy and there was no sound from within. She could turn back, no one need know what she had witnessed, and it had been nearly dark so perhaps she had been mistaken. Then there was the trouble she might get in, promises that had been made. No, something wasn't right here and maybe if she found out what was going on her parents would be proud for once and would get off her case.

Taking a deep breath Rosie tiptoed carefully up the narrow path, acutely aware of every crack and rustle that her white trainers made, sounds seeming magnified in the darkness. The trees leaned in, blocking all but the occasional burst of light that dared to trespass here, equally as unwelcome as her. There was a flicker of a torch ahead, a man's voice. Rosie froze, had they seen her? She crept forward warily and soon found herself at the edge of the wood, the bunker ahead of her. Dark figures were entering it from the far end. A door slammed. Rosie waited to be sure they had gone, then, keeping to the tree line, she went to the end of the bunker. There was a heavy metal door, too thick to hear any sound, so taking a breath she left the safety of the trees and climbed the overgrown grassy bank that led up over the top of the bunker and walked along to one of the protruding chimney structures. There were two thin metal bars near the top that formed a cross over the hole, and below that was a dim glow of light. She could hear voices.

'Stop yer snivelling,' came the echo of a man's voice through the hollow space beneath.

'She don't like the dark,' came a quiet voice.

Rosie's heart lurched; that sounded like a child's voice. A girl, she guessed.

'It's better camouflage for your sort, you should be used to it from the jungle.' The man laughed.

Rosie gritted her teeth, her lips forming a hard angry line. There was scuffling and then the light went out.

'Sleep well, kiddies, you got a long journey ahead of you tomorrow,' cackled the man.

Rosie heard muffled voices in another part of the bunker. She left the hole she was listening by and crossed to the other. The voices were clearer there.

'…tomorrow morning. All twelve of them are going to London this time. We've had big orders coming in, so we're going to have to step up the workload.'

Rosie recognised the cold, emotionless voice of the blond man she'd seen earlier.

'Give us some of that.'

'I think you've had enough.'

'I don't think that's up to you. Just because Gabriel's not in 'ere doesn't make you the boss.'

'Go and pack up the shit before I slam your head into that concrete wall.'

'Arrghhh.'

Rosie heard a scuffle. Then silence.

'You go and help him, Griff.'

''Ello pretty.' Rosie leapt sideways, nearly falling backwards down the bank, stopped only by a large hand around her neck that dragged her to her feet. Hot breath, rancid with alcohol, caressed her face.

'We don't usually bag ourselves a little white girl but I'm sure we can make an exception.'

The voice was soft and silvery, a contrast to the bulk of the man that towered over her. Rosie's head was screaming at her legs to move but they refused to pay attention, and before she had time to berate them for their lack of urgency she was being dragged down the bank and into the bunker.

The blond man was leaning against the wall as they entered, a glass in his hand.

'Get your stinking hands off me!' screamed Rosie, finally finding her voice.

Rosie thought she saw a flicker of fear in the blond man's eyes as he looked her up and down.

'What you got there, Gabriel?' asked the short hairy man that Rosie remembered was called Rusty, as he entered the room carrying plastic cups and a water bottle.

'An addition to our little party,' replied Gabriel, shoving Rosie forward so the others could inspect her closely.

'Not bad.' Rusty snorted, slithering up to Rosie and sniffing her. Rosie shrank back from his watery lips as they brushed her cheek.

'That's enough, Rusty,' said the blond man, pushing him out of the way. 'Where'd you find her?' he asked, walking around Rosie and looking her up and down.

'She was listening on the roof when I came back from the truck,' said Gabriel, pouring himself a drink.

'What are we supposed to do with her?' asked the blond man, holding his glass out for a refill.

'We'll have to take her with us to London, what choice do we have?'

'I can think of something we can do with her,' Rusty smiled, licking his lips.

'I thought I told you to get on with packing the shit up!' exploded the blond man.

Rusty scuttled out of the room, muttering.

'Is that a good idea?' asked the blond man, returning his attention to Gabriel. 'We said we were going to stay away from white Brits coz they attract too much attention and there's always someone who will look for them.'

'Well we don't have any choice, Zaydain. There's no point doing away with her here, we may as well get some work out of her,' said Gabriel. 'Besides, the amount of money we can get for her will be worth the risk. You should be celebrating.'

'The place will be crawling with cops! They're not gonna let this one get away; think of the publicity she will draw. We'll all be finished!' shouted Zaydain, pacing the room. 'She must have a family who will care if she doesn't come home tonight, and that's no good for us. No one is looking for them others, no one cares that they haven't come home, but this one… You said no white girls, Gabriel, that was the deal. Black don't show the dirt.'

'Grow some, Zaydain! This was never gonna be a church picnic. This is business.'

Rosie was finding it hard to follow the conversation; there was a ringing in her ears like a fire alarm. It chased the fear as it started its slow torturous journey from the top of her head down into her stomach and then out to her arms and legs. She wanted her mummy; she needed to go now.

'Please, I need to go home,' she whispered. 'I won't say anything, I promise. I'll pretend none of this happened. It will be like I was never here.'

Gabriel's laugh was deep as it rattled around his huge, muscular body. Rosie's legs started to shake. 'As far as we're concerned, you're not here, love. You're a no one, a nobody, a piece of fine-cut meat to be sold on to the highest bidder,' he said, moving closer to her. He put his hands around her throat and whispered in her ear. 'It will make a nice change to have a bit of white meat on the menu.'

# Chapter 4

There was a knock at his bedroom door. Ted peeled himself off the bed and went to turn down his music.

'Sorry!' he said, knowing it would be his mum telling him it was too loud. 'Lost track of time,' he said guiltily, looking at his clock that said eleven thirty.

'Is Rosie with you?' came his mum's voice through the door. Ted was about to say no, then paused. Was she not in her room? Surely she didn't... He wasn't going to cover for her again, not this time!

'Yes,' he heard himself say. 'We're just listening to some music.'

'Well, it's late, so ten more minutes, OK?'

'Sure thing, Mum.' Ted winced at the lie.

FUCK!

Ted looked out of the window into the pitch of the night. Surely she didn't go on her own. She hated the dark. But she could have gone hours ago, while it was still light, in which case, why wasn't she back? Fear gripped his throat like a livid crab. He had to tell his parents. But then Rosie would never forgive him. FUCK! How could she do this, after everything?

He paced back and forth across the bedroom, his head a pounding contradiction of choices: Go looking for Rosie; 'fess up to his parents; or do nothing until the morning and hope Rosie showed up. In the past he would have gone looking for her when she didn't come home, cover for her to their parents, at least until it became obvious things were at crisis point. But Rosie had made a promise to all of them since then, and if she couldn't stick to her side than neither would he. He threw himself down on his bed, decision made. She would have to learn that some of the responsibility lay with her, he wasn't always going to come and rescue her, not anymore.

Despite feeling confident in his tough-love decision, all the worst case scenarios flicked through his mind like a badly edited movie. As he closed his eyes, Ted pictured her being dragged from the forest by a ten-foot-tall pirate with seaweed for hair. He had her under his arm and was running towards the water, giant strides eating up the beach and leaving craters where his feet had been. As the man reached the breaking waves, he flung Rosie onto his back and broke the water's surface with a huge splash, taking Rosie down with him into the murky depths.

Ted awoke to the sun streaming through his window. For a brief moment all was well with the world, until he noticed he was fully clothed. He flew out of his room and along the corridor towards Rosie's room, his heart pounding, a prayer on his lips. He flung her bedroom door open so hard that it slammed against the wall.

'What are you doing?' asked his mum, appearing from her room, her arms laden with clothes.

Ted just stared at the empty bed in front of him.

'Ted?' came his mum's voice, more urgently. 'What's going on?'

Ted couldn't turn around; he couldn't look his mum in the eye and tell her he'd let them all down.

'Ted!' said his mum again with more aggression.

He turned around slowly, knowing his mum would read his expression in an instant.

'Oh my God, what's happened?' she shrieked, dropping the clothes and shaking him by the shoulders. Ted's eyes fell to the floor.

'What's wrong with you? Speak to me, goddam it!' His mum was reaching hysteria as Ted searched desperately for the right words. He knew his silence was creating its own horror in his mum's mind, but he just didn't know where to begin.

'What's going on?' asked his dad, appearing from downstairs.

'Something's happened to Rosie, Sam, and Ted won't speak,' she shrieked in frustration.

'Ted,' came his dad's rational voice from amidst the screaming, 'where's your sister?'

Ted looked into his dad's eyes and saw the calm that he needed. He started from the beginning and told them what had happened.

His mum started crying as Ted relayed the events of the day before.

'Everyone just keep cool,' said his dad. 'We don't know that anything has happened to her. There's no need to jump to the worst conclusions, there are a thousand explanations for why she didn't come home last night and we're not going to assume that the right one is the most sinister, not yet. This isn't London, what can actually happen to her in the depths of the countryside? She probably just stayed out last night to prove a point, to punish us for making her move here.'

Ted was grateful for his dad's calm reasoning but there was no escaping the underlying panic that they all felt.

'Bella,' Sam said, taking her in his arms. 'You will stay here in case Rosie calls or comes back, and phone the police. Ted and I will go to the beach and bunker and see whether she's just decided to hang out there for the night. You know what she's like and she was frustrated yesterday. We will find her, whatever it takes, so you mustn't worry.'

Bella nodded at Sam and then glanced at Ted. Ted couldn't read her eyes but they weren't forgiving, and he knew that if he didn't make amends for his failings as a brother and son then he would never find forgiveness in them again.

They half ran, half stumbled down the cliff towards the beach. Great dust clouds plumed behind them as they slipped and slid on the loose surface. Reaching the bottom in a few minutes they looked around, unsure which way to go. The sun was still just a halo of light behind the cliffs that cast imposing shadows across the beach. Ted pulled his coat around him unsure if it was the chill of the departing night or the eeriness of what lay before them that made him shiver.

'Where should we start?' came his dad's shaking voice as he panted next to him.

'Well she mentioned a wooded area when she told me about the bunker she found, so maybe we should start there,' replied Ted, pointing towards the trees to their right. His dad nodded and they both crunched their way along the beach.

Even in the daylight the wood was heavy with green shadows and Ted wondered if his little sister had walked this same path last night, groping her way in the darkness, alone. Why hadn't he just agreed to go with her? She was only fourteen; a mature fourteen-year-old, granted, but still his little sister.

'Rosie!' Ted found himself shouting.

'Ted, I don't think we should shout; we have no idea if those men are still here,' hissed his dad.

'But what if she fell and is lying injured somewhere in this wood?'

'Let's at least suss out the area first and make sure there's no one else here, then we can shout, OK?'

They broke the edge of the woods and came face to face with a concrete building.

'That must be the bunker thing Rosie talked about,' said Ted.

'It definitely is a bunker, it looks like an old communication centre or a look-out that would have been used in the Second World War,' said his dad, walking around it.

'Is there a way in? This path seems to lead back towards the house. Although where it widens here, it could lead to a road in the other direction.'

'There's a way in here,' shouted his dad from the other side.

Ted followed the voice around to the left end of the bunker. There was a metal barred gate set into two sloping concrete walls that created a porch. His dad was struggling with the gate.

'It won't open, there's a padlock,' he said, rattling it as though that would loosen it.

'Well she can't be in there then,' said Ted. 'ROSIE!' he shouted. 'ROSIE! ROSIE!' It felt good to be able to shout and his dad joined in. 'Look,' said Ted suddenly. 'Someone has been here; there are cigarette butts everywhere. And these nettles look well trampled.' He looked around for a rock and found a rusty metal bar. 'Here, let me try.' Ted banged it against the padlock as hard as he could. It felt good to be hitting something hard. It took a few blows before the padlock gave way and fell to the floor.

Ted swung the gate open and stepped cautiously inside. There was a wall directly in front of the gate so he turned left and then immediately right and entered a room. It was a concrete box; four walls, a floor and a ceiling, all grey. There was some graffiti and the walls were crumbling at the edges. It reminded Ted of a public toilet, but without the cubicles and wash basins. The only light was coming from the ceiling where a chimney-like structure led out of the top, crossed at the opening by two metal bars.

Ted looked around, desperately searching for signs of Rosie. All he could see were a few bits of rubbish, an old paper cup, and a few nails. It smelt of people: a mixture of urine, sweat, breath, stale food and alcohol. It was as if he could still feel a presence: a lingering past slow to catch up with its future.

'Were you here, Rosie?' he whispered, squatting down.

'Nothing in there,' said his dad, walking in. 'Just another concrete room like this but smaller. A few old cigarette butts scattered around but nothing else. You found anything in here?'

'No,' said Ted, looking up. 'Are there any other rooms?'

'No, just these two. I don't think she was here, Ted. Come on, let's head back up the path, see if we can find anything else.'

'OK, Dad, just give me a minute.'

He knew his dad was trying to be strong and positive for him, but they'd been here before, many times, and the disappointment that nothing had changed, even way out here, was evident in his voice.

Ted glanced around the room once more. If Rosie had been here there was no sign of her now. As much as he'd hated the idea of finding evidence of her being in the bunker, it was the only place he thought he might find her. Where else could she be? He looked down as a spider crawled past his foot, its long legs searching out the safest route. And then he saw it. Something etched into the concrete. He changed his position so the light was shining fully onto it. It was a picture of a cigarette lighter; roughly done but definitely a lighter, Ted was sure of it. He stared at it. Where had he seen a lighter like that before? It wasn't unusual by any means, a common Clipper lighter, he'd used one the same many times, but it sparked a memory in his mind. He traced the image with his finger; there was still dust around it from the engraving. Could that mean it had been done recently?

Suddenly Ted jumped up. He knew where he'd seen that lighter before, but he had to be sure. He ran out of the bunker, shouting as he passed his dad, 'I have to go home, I'll meet you there.'

# Chapter 5

Rosie hugged her knees tightly as the truck rumbled and shook around her. Twenty-seven pairs of frightened eyes glinted in the semi-dark, some looking at her, some focussed on a faraway place, anywhere but here. Rosie caught the eye of the girl opposite who was cradling a smaller girl. She smiled at Rosie. It was the first contact Rosie had had with anyone since she'd been thrown into the room with them all the night before, and although it was just a smile, it coated her fear in reassurance and muffled her pounding heart.

Rosie thought about her family for what felt like the hundredth time since she'd been captured. She could only imagine how worried they must be, not to mention angry with her for running off like she did. And Ted was probably taking the brunt of it for not stopping her when he had the chance. Guilt lay in the pit of her stomach like a coiled snake.

'I was in a truck like this once before when it was full of birds. If you were a bird, what kind of bird would you be?'

Rosie looked up in surprise; the girl who had smiled was looking at her expectantly, then when Rosie didn't reply, continued, 'I'd be a parrot. They are great imitators, have beautiful bright feathers, and they are shipped around the world to live in elaborate houses and be loved by kind rich people.'

For a moment Rosie just stared, confused by the fact that she understood what the girl was saying before realising she was in fact speaking English, if with a slight accent, and it wasn't that Rosie had slipped into a parallel universe.

'Umm, I guess I'd be a pigeon,' replied Rosie at last, not wanting to be unfriendly.

'Yes, amazing birds, very intelligent and very underestimated,' enthused the girl.

That wasn't exactly why Rosie had chosen a pigeon; more because she thought they were chubby, rather plain and uninteresting birds, considered a pest.

'Really?' replied Rosie.

'Yes, they're quite remarkable. They can find their way home in one day from as far away as six-hundred miles. Some people believe they use roads and motorways to navigate, others say they use the earth's magnetic field and landmarks, and even the sun. They are the most intelligent of all birds. It was a good choice,' said the girl.

Rosie was aware she was still staring; mouth agape.

'How do you know all this stuff?' Rosie asked.

'Oh, my dad sells exotic birds,' she replied.

The truck suddenly swung to the side and screeched to a halt. All the children in the back screamed as they were flung against each other. Rosie was ripped from the surreal conversation she was having and dropped firmly back into the horror of where she was, hitting her shoulder hard in the process. There was a lot of shouting outside before the truck started moving again.

Rosie looked around her. No one seemed to be too badly hurt, just a few bruises and tears. Then the bird girl began to sing.

*Thula, thula, thula, Mtwana*
*Thula, thula, thula, Mtwana*
*Ungakhali*

*Umama akekho*

*Umama uzobuya*
*Be still, be still, be still, my child*

*Be still, be still, be still, my child*
*Do not cry*

*Mother is absent*
*Mother shall come back.*

Rosie rubbed her bruised shoulder as she listened to the soothing voice. She couldn't tell from looking at her how old the girl was. Her sad hazel eyes and drawn face reflected a history, life experiences; but her thin childlike body and smooth dark skin had no stories to tell. She was wearing a brightly coloured dress, one that Rosie thought would have been saved for a special occasion, and in her hair she had a sparkly clip in the same shades: red, green, yellow, blue. In their dingy surroundings Rosie thought she provided a splash of coloured hope and it was reassuring to look at her.

The girl in her arms was smaller. She looked younger but her skin wasn't smooth; her legs and arms were covered in pink scars. She was whimpering like a distressed animal; it was unnerving and Rosie wished she would stop.

'She's had a hard time,' said the bird girl as if reading her thoughts.

Rosie realised she had been staring. 'Sorry. Yes, poor thing, she must be really frightened,' she said quickly.

'They all are. It's hard when you don't know what's happening or where you're going. None of them speaks English so it's confusing for them. My name's Baduwa by the way.'

'I'm Rosie. How come you speak such good English?'

'English is the official language of Nigeria, but I speak it especially well because my father is English. He insisted that I learn what he called the Queen's English because he said it would help me get places. It seems he was right, look where I am!'

'He knows you're here?' asked Rosie, surprised and a little unnerved.

'Oh yes, it was his idea that I should come to Europe and find a better life for myself, one he couldn't give me.' She smiled.

Rosie looked away, unable to look at this strange girl who seemed to be unnervingly happy about where they were. Instead she stared at the frightened faces around her, sure her own face mirrored theirs, the one consolation that she was still home, still in England, a place that was familiar to her, where there were laws and justice. These children probably had no idea where they were, or whether they would ever see their families again.

The truck had slowed down, was stopping and starting, and Rosie heard sounds that meant they could only be in London. Under any normal circumstances she would have been excited about being home, but now that her family wasn't here she wasn't sure it was home anymore, and she longed to be where her family were right now more than anything in the world.

Suddenly Rosie felt a small hand creeping into hers. She looked down and saw a little Chinese boy looking up at her. Trying to pull her hand away, embarrassed by this strange boy's attention, she looked at Baduwa.

'I think his name is Lo,' said Baduwa. 'It's the only thing he's said since he got here. He arrived with the last group of children, those two there, and her,' she said, pointing to three others.

'I don't understand,' said Rosie. 'What could they want with all these children?'

'Don't you know?' asked Baduwa, looking surprised.

Suddenly the truck screeched to a halt, doors slammed then a stream of bright light flooded the children as the back was opened. Rosie felt Lo crouch down behind her, hiding from the intimidating silhouettes that loomed in the doorway. Rosie recoiled, ready to bite and claw anyone who tried to touch her, but it was three other children who were dragged aggressively out of the back of the truck before the door was pulled shut with a bang.

Rosie wrapped her arms around her bended legs and made herself as small as she could. Some of the children crawled closer to the back of the truck. Baduwa didn't move. Her confidence was beginning to freak Rosie out; she seemed so completely unperturbed by what was happening around her as she hummed quietly, gently rocking the girl still wrapped in her arms.

The truck started up again, and although that came with its own slight reassurance, Rosie couldn't shake the picture of the way those children were pulled from the truck, aggressively, coldly, like pieces of meat. And then she remembered what Gabriel had said: *You're a no one, a nobody, a piece of fine-cut meat to be sold on to the highest bidder.* Is that what was happening to all these children, to her? Were they being sold like meat to a butcher?

She looked accusingly at Baduwa.

'Do you know what's happening to us?' she hissed.

Baduwa looked a bit taken aback by Rosie's sudden aggression. 'Well I know what's happening to me and I assume the same goes for everyone else,' she replied.

'What exactly is happening to you? What are you doing here?'

'I'm here to get a good job, study if I want to. I've been promised a nice house, some starting out money, a better life for myself. I have to pay back the money my journey cost but it won't take long once I have a good job.'

'Who promised you all of this?' asked Rosie, digging her nails into the palm of her hand.

'A man. He said he'd been watching me, thought I was wasted in Nigeria and that there was so much more waiting for me in Europe. I'd always wanted to see where my dad came from so of course I jumped at the chance to come here. He spoke to my dad and everything first, got his permission. He was so nice, so complimentary, bought me clothes and jewellery,' she rushed, suddenly sensing Rosie's alarm. 'It's OK, we had a commitment ceremony; we are bound, and so protected.'

'Where is he now?' Rosie asked, quietly.

'He said he'd meet me here; said he'd find me.'

The truck stopped again. The back door was raised and two more children were pulled out. Rosie opened her mouth to scream but nothing would come out. Climbing over the other children she scrambled towards the closing door. *I can't stay here!* she screamed silently, putting her hand out to stop it sliding shut, but she was too slow and it closed with a bang, leaving her breathless and crying whilst the truck started up again and moved off.

# Chapter 6

Ted threw open his bedroom door and ran over to his CD collection that was stacked neatly in his bookcase. He rifled through, tossing the rejections onto his bed. Then he found what he was looking for. He slumped down on the chair by his bed staring at the cover of The Streets album. He leaned forward and grabbed another, then another; it was there on each one: the Clipper lighter.

He knew immediately what it meant: it was the one passion they shared, the one thing that brought brother and sister together despite everything else that was going on in their lives; their love of The Streets. It became their lodestar, their signature band. For them it represented London and their lives there. And when everything got too much they each had a headphone ear-piece, and lost themselves in the music together. And that was why she'd engraved the picture; his little sister had been taken to London, back to the one place in the world she wanted to be, but for all the wrong reasons.

Ted slammed his fist hard against the wall, his face contorting in agony, then threw the CDs across the room, rage and fear filling him up until he was ready to explode. London was such a vast city, how would he find her? He collapsed onto the floor, head in his hands.

'Ted?' His mum stood in the doorway. She looked older, afraid.

'I think she's in London, Mum,' Ted said quietly. He then told her how they'd found the bunker, what it was like, and the picture of the lighter. He pointed weakly at one of the CDs on the floor. His mum walked over and picked one up.

'This lighter? Are you sure?' she asked, stroking the cover.

'I think so, at least that's all I have to go on. It makes sense.'

'We have to tell the police everything, you'll have to tell them *everything*,' she whispered.

'Sure, Mum, whatever it takes.'

'They should be here soon.' She walked out, leaving a trail of sadness in her wake.

Ted lay on his bed curling his knees up under his chin, his head pounding. Rosie's face appeared behind his eyelids but then she turned away and started running, weaving in and out of the streets of London, always just a little bit out of reach. As he chased her, each street became narrower and narrower until only she could fit down them; he was too big to squeeze through. He pushed at the walls with all his might but they wouldn't budge. She looked back, saw that he couldn't follow and stopped. Her face was drenched in disappointment and pity. She ran on and disappeared out of sight. Ted sat up, breathing heavily.

He felt someone in the room and looked around. His dad was standing in the doorway. He walked over to where one of The Streets albums lay on the floor. He picked it up, stroking the cover like Ted's mum had.

'Are you sure about this London thing, Ted?' he asked.

'No, I'm not sure, but I have a strong feeling that's where she is. She'd have known I would come looking, like always…' He gasped at the pain of those words because if he'd gone looking sooner, like she would have assumed, this wouldn't be happening. 'And she would have found a way to let me know where she was going to be, I just know it.' He paused. 'I don't know who's got her or why, and the worst part is we have no way of knowing how long she'll be there…' he paused again. 'So I need to go… today, now.'

'What? No, we should wait for the police to organise a hunt.'

'It's my fault, Dad. And I can't wait around hoping the police will find her. I have to do something now. I know people, Dad, people who can help. Many eyes are better than a few.'

Ted waited for his dad to say no, but all he did was look at Ted and sigh.

'I'm not sure your mum will be happy to have both of you out of her sight but I'll talk to her,' he said, sitting down on the bed and wrapping his arms around Ted. They sat there for what seemed like ages.

Then Ted heard a car pull into the drive.


Detective Sanders and PC Jones sat at the kitchen table drinking tea and asking a million questions as Ted tried to be as helpful as he could, all the time twitching on the edge of his seat, desperate to get going. The police dredged up the past, wanting to know everything about Rosie, and Ted could see the flicker of suspicion in their eyes when his mum mentioned all the trouble that Rosie had been in, as if that suddenly added a whole other explanation as to where she might be, and why. As PC Jones scribbled in her notebook, Ted resisted the urge to grab it off her and cross out that part, like he could cross out that bit of Rosie's life. He knew that if he became difficult about it, the whole process would just take longer and he stood a much better chance of finding her than they did, anyway. He knew London and he knew people who could get into places the police couldn't, people who knew how to get at the mechanics of London; turn up the pressure, turn down the heat.

The detective got on his radio and instructed the person on the other end to send out forensics. They wanted Ted to show them the bunker, see if they could get some fingerprints, and look at the picture of the lighter that Rosie had carved.

Ted looked at his dad, pleadingly.

'Detective, I went with Ted to the bunker, do you think it would be possible for me to show it to you. Ted's had very little sleep and I think he needs to rest.'

His mum looked questioningly at his dad, and he took her hand and squeezed it. The detective nodded and agreed that it would probably be best if Sam went anyway. Ted smiled at his mum and dad and then shook the detective's hand.

'Anything else you need to ask me, don't hesitate to call,' said Ted.

Ted left the room and sprinted up the stairs to pack. He threw some clothes into his bag, his iPod, wallet, phone. He saw one of The Streets CDs lying on the floor. He picked it up and looked at the cover. 'I'm coming, Rosie,' he whispered. He threw the CD into his bag and looked around the room for anything he'd forgotten. His eyes fell on a pile of loose photos sitting on his chest of drawers. He picked them up, thumbing through until he found a recent one of Rosie sitting on the steps of their old house. She looked so young; her chin resting on top of her knees, the sun warming her pale skin, her full lips slightly turned down at the corners. Ted had never noticed that faraway look in her eyes before, like she wanted to be somewhere else, or someone else. But how long would it be before they reverted to that look again now that she was back in London? He had to find her before that happened.

Ted turned to put the picture in his bag and saw his mum standing in the doorway.

'They've left. Your father said to take you to the train station,' she said. 'Are you sure you know what you're doing? I don't think I could stand to lose both my children.'

Ted walked over to his mum and tentatively put his arms around her. She rested her head on his chest and Ted could hear her breathing him in.

'I have to do something, Mum. I can't just sit around here waiting, not when it's my fault.'

'It's not your fault, Ted. You've spent your whole life looking out for your little sister, I know that,' she whispered.

'She'd promised to grow up, take responsibility for her own actions. You weren't to know this would happen.'

She pulled away from him and took a deep breath. 'Your father and I will come to London too, as soon as he gets back, and stay at Uncle Jim's. Will you be at Dillon's?'

'Yes. I haven't asked him yet but he said I could anytime.'

'OK, well let's go then.' She picked up Ted's bag.

'I've got that, Mum,' he said, taking it off her.

As they walked out of his room, Ted realised he had no idea when he'd be back and, strangely, felt sad to be leaving. London suddenly seemed sinister and dark, a place that bad things gravitated to, and he wasn't sure he wanted to go back there anymore, not like this.

# Chapter 7

Rosie rolled over. Someone was snoring so loudly it was like being in a room with a lawnmower. Ted? She kicked out her leg, hoping to make contact with whomever it was. Nothing. She tried again, a little to the left. Still nothing. Where the hell was he?

'Ted, shut up!' she finally shouted, throwing her pillow into the darkness.

'Rosie? You OK?'

Rosie jumped.

'It's alright, you're dreaming.'

Baduwa crawled across the floor and sat on what Rosie now remembered was a dirty old mattress on the floor of a filthy flat somewhere in London. The snoring was coming from Utibe.

Baduwa stroked Rosie's hair and hummed quietly as Rosie looked across at the fourth mattress with a small lump in the middle she knew to be Lo. The truck had made more stops before bringing the four of them to a part of London she didn't know. They'd walked up five flights of stairs to the top floor of a low-rise block of flats, the setting sun colouring their ascent orange. The door they'd entered was the last in a row of seven doors, all covered with graffiti. Dirty net curtains hung in the even dirtier windows. They'd been pushed into a tiny room with four mattresses littering the stained floor, and four blankets in a pile in the corner. Paint was peeling off the walls like loose scabs, and the smell was a mixture of damp and urine. Having not slept at all the night before, they'd all crashed out, hoping to escape to the blissful peace that sleep brought.

'What were you dreaming about?' asked Baduwa, tucking her legs up under her dress and hugging them.

'I heard snoring and thought it was my brother Ted,' Rosie replied, pulling the blanket up under her chin. It smelt of sick.

'Oh, you have a brother? I have three at home in Nigeria.' Baduwa smiled into the darkness.

'Do you miss it? Nigeria, I mean,' asked Rosie.

'Not yet. I thought I would, having lived there my whole fourteen years, but I'm so excited about what's waiting for me here.'

Rosie was surprised they were the same age because Baduwa looked so much older than she did. Rosie still felt like a very frightened child much too far away from home, and yet Baduwa was much further away from her home but she didn't seem to mind.

'Wow, your parents must be really chilled, mine never let me go anywhere on my own, not anymore,' Rosie said.

'Children grow up quickly where I come from,' Baduwa replied, looking down at her feet and picking at a painted toenail. 'I'm one of the lucky ones, my parents cared about me enough to help me to leave, Utibe's parents too, but the ones that are still there, I don't know...' She trailed off and turned her attention to her hair, adjusting the clip. 'What I wouldn't give for a mirror right now, I must look dreadful.' She sighed.

Rosie frowned at her; something wasn't right with this picture. Baduwa seemed so sure that she was going to get this great house and a job, but Rosie could see no evidence of that so far. And she doubted very much that the men who had brought them there were humanitarians.

Rosie looked across the room as Utibe began to stir; sitting up, she too looked around, as if surprised by where she was. Her vacant eyes fell on Rosie and Baduwa and she climbed off her mattress and wandered over, her head down, hands playing with the front of her brown dress. Baduwa opened her arms and Utibe crawled onto her lap and snuggled into her.

'She doesn't say much, does she?' observed Rosie.

'Probably because she can't,' replied Baduwa.

'Yeah, you said she doesn't speak English, but I thought she might speak her own language occasionally.'

'She would if she could, but she can't speak at all.'

'Oh,' said Rosie, looking at the tiny body curled on Baduwa's knee. 'What, not at all? Ever?'

'She used to speak, of course, but she has no tongue,' replied Baduwa, stroking Utibe's hair.

'What? Where is it?' Rosie asked, instantly regretting the ridiculous question that made it sound like Utibe had been careless and merely misplaced it somewhere.

'It was taken, of course,' replied Baduwa, shaking her head at Rosie's apparent ignorance. 'You know, cut out. Removed.'

Rosie suddenly felt like a naïve child, not privy to the experiences the rest of them shared. After all, she was an impostor, an uninvited guest.

'But why?' asked Rosie, confused.

'You really know nothing about what goes on outside of your white little world, do you?' Baduwa sighed.

Rosie felt like she'd been slapped round the face. She put both her hands up and touched her cheeks reflexively, feeling hurt but more ashamed at her ignorance. Tears threatened to escape from her eyes and she squeezed them shut, burying her face under the smelly blanket, mortified by her weakness. But she couldn't contain the flow and soon gave in and let herself cry for her mum and dad, for Ted, for getting caught, for her uncertain future, for Lo, Baduwa and Utibe and for all the other children that had been pulled off that truck and were living their own little piece of hell.

Rosie felt a hand on her head and the blanket pulled gently away; her hot, swollen eyes met Utibe's. Rosie hated herself, she had nothing to cry about compared to this poor girl, and yet Utibe was soothing her with a timid smile that she must have struggled so hard to find after everything that had happened to her.

Rosie wiped the tears ashamedly from her cheeks and smiled back. 'I'm sorry, I don't know where all that came from. Thanks, Utibe.' She nodded, taking her hand and squeezing it.

'Don't worry, we've all done it, many times,' said Baduwa, getting to her feet. 'Do you suppose they'll feed us soon?' she asked, walking to a window and peering out into the slowly breaking dawn. 'I wonder what time it is.'

Rosie desperately wanted to ask more about Utibe but decided she'd said enough wrong things for one day, so kept her mouth shut, instead watching Baduwa gaze at herself in the faint reflection of the window. Suddenly it occurred to her that they hadn't even tried to escape, to see if there was a way out. Getting slowly to her feet, she walked casually to the door, pressed the handle down and pushed; it didn't budge. Another door led to a bathroom but as Rosie opened the door and cast around the dark little room – toilet with broken seat, stained shower cubicle – she found no window. Walking casually to the window next to the one Baduwa was now preening herself in, Rosie banged feebly at the thick glass held in place by windows that were clearly new in comparison to the squalor of the rest of the building. She watched people rushing about below, beginning their day like everything was well with the world; so near and yet so unaware of what was unfolding just a few feet away.

'They won't hear you,' said Baduwa, pulling her hair tight and fastening the clip. 'And even if they could, do you really think they would care?'

Rosie felt a small hand creep into hers and looked down to see Lo's wide brown eyes looking up at her, searching her face for a smile, for some sort of reassurance. Rosie put her arm around him and from somewhere deep inside found the smile she knew he so desperately needed. If only someone would give her the same comfort. The tears threatened to fall again so she rubbed her eyes fiercely, pushing them back inside, and started to pace. Pacing always seemed to work in movies; for some reason it magically produced an idea as if the movement dislodged it from its hiding place and sent it drifting upwards like a bubble until it popped on the surface, bursting with ideas. She walked from one side of the small room to the other, turning the situation over in her mind, as six eyes watched her expectantly.

Firstly, they still had no idea what the kidnappers wanted with them. Secondly, even if they were all prepared to make a break for it, which she doubted, the four of them could never overpower fully-grown men. Thirdly, the windows were all locked and virtually soundproof, so there was no way of attracting anyone else's attention. And, finally, and most frustratingly, in her haste to leave the house she had forgotten her phone. It seemed the bubble was not ready to be dislodged just yet, after all. She would have to bide her time and hope something presented itself. For now the only hope was that Ted had found the clue and understood it.

A key turning in the door interrupted Rosie's thoughts. Lo ran over and hid behind her and Rosie rested her hand protectively on his skinny shoulder, bracing herself for what came next. Only one man came through the door and Rosie recognised him as the slightly strange quiet one she'd seen from her hiding place beside the bunker; Griff she thought his name was. He was carrying a tray of food, which he placed awkwardly on the ground just inside the door. His eyes fixed firmly on the floor; Rosie saw her chance.

'Why are you keeping us here?' she demanded. Griff shook his head and started to leave the room but Rosie leapt across the mattress and grabbed his arm. He could easily have shaken her off or struck her but he merely froze, his eyes averted.

'Please,' she said quietly. 'Just tell us what you're going to do with us. My family will be so worried.' Her voice started to break and she released her grip on Griff's arm and took a step back. Refusing to look at her he shook his head slowly and then left the room, locking the door behind him.

Rosie watched, alarmed, as the others raced to the tray and began devouring the food on it. She really didn't feel that hungry, despite the empty pain in her stomach, and there was no telling what was in the greeny-brown-coloured stew they were eating. But when Utibe held out a bowl to her she took it, slowly lifting a spoonful up to her mouth and gagging at the smell of stale cabbages and vinegar. Rosie shook her head guiltily, reaching for a crust of bread instead. It was like eating a furry piece of crumbling concrete but at least it didn't reek of vomit. Baduwa picked up the discarded bowl and gave the rest to Utibe and Lo, and despite not one word passing between them Rosie felt the gaping jaw of equivalence stretch ever wider.

Just then the key turned in the door. This time it wasn't Griff, it was the blond man, Zaydain, and he wasn't alone. Standing behind him was another man that Rosie didn't recognise. He wore glasses on top of a sweating bulbous nose, and was bald except for a few wisps of brown hair that lay carefully across the top of his red head. His suit struggled to meet across his wheezing chest, and his eyes glistened moist with interest as he gazed at the four of them.

Rosie cringed as his eyes swung round to her but they quickly returned to Lo and he nodded at Zaydain.

Zaydain stepped forward to grab Lo but Rosie leapt in his way, shielding Lo, pushing him behind her. 'What are you doing with him? Where are you taking him?' she screamed. Unlike Griff, Zaydain had no trouble looking her in the eyes and as he did he pushed Rosie roughly out of the way and grabbed Lo by his shirt, dragging him out of the room, his little body hanging from Zaydain's grip like a rag doll. Rosie jumped to her feet and raced towards the door, tears streaming down her face. She was already failing to protect him, despite her reassurance that everything would be OK. Lo looked back as he was dragged away, his eyes wide with fear, his arms stretched out towards her, a silent scream on his lips. Rosie let out a long, terrified scream of her own and threw herself against the door as it slammed in her face, pummelling it angrily with her feeble fists. But he was gone.

# Chapter 8

'Just couldn't stay away, eh, mate?' Dillon laughed as he held the door open for Ted. 'Missed me too much, I know. It's OK, nothing to be embarrassed about.'

Ted smiled. Dillon always made him feel better. As he walked into the familiar living room, he could hear Dillon's mum singing to the radio in the kitchen. It was one of the sounds of his youth and it made him feel nostalgic to hear it after what seemed like forever. He'd spent a lot of time at Dillon's growing up, mostly when tensions were high at home because of some incident involving Rosie; all the kids gravitated there thanks to Dillon's mum's warmth and understanding. Not to mention her famous chocolate brownies.

'Are you sure your mum doesn't mind me staying?' asked Ted, sinking into an armchair.

'Are you kidding? She loves having you around, thinks you're a good influence on me for some reason. If only she knew the truth, eh?' Dillon laughed, sitting in the chair opposite. 'Now, tell me what's going on.'

Ted began the long story of the past few days. Dillon listened without interruption; his face unreadable. As he spoke, Ted felt emotion welling inside himself, but it wasn't the despair and sadness he'd felt back at home, it was anger, raw and savage. Now that he was back in London, the place he considered to be his true home, Ted felt betrayed by it.

Suddenly the place he'd trusted with his life had revealed its true identity; it was a place that bred dishonesty and greed. Well, he decided, it owed him, and he was going to use every piece of knowledge and every contact he had to reach inside its festering bowels and pull his sister out.

Ted suddenly realised that he was standing and gesticulating wildly, shouting about how he was going to kill whoever had taken his little sister, Dillon watching him passively from the chair. He sat back down and smiled sheepishly and Dillon shook his head not in judgement but disbelief.

Just then Dillon's mum walked in. 'Ted!' she boomed. 'I thought I heard voices.' She waddled over and planted a beer beside each of them. Ted couldn't help grinning at her happy face; she was always pleased to see him. Her tiny eyes sparkled, as she looked him up and down.

'Still need to put some weight on you.' She laughed, her own ample body bouncing in agreement.

'Hey, Mrs M,' said Ted. 'Are you sure it's OK if I stay for a few days?'

'Always so polite, you hear that, Dillon?' she said, cuffing him playfully round the head.

'Yeah, yeah, he's such a gent,' replied Dillon, rolling his eyes.

'Of course, darlin', stay as long as you like, give me a chance to fatten you up.' She laughed again, patting her own belly.

Ted lifted his beer in Dillon's direction as Mrs M left the room. 'Up yer bum!' he said, taking a swig.

Dillon nodded. 'Up yours.' Then he shook his head again. 'I can't believe it, mate, how could this have happened? You only just left! Well, no point wasting time on the whys, the first thing we're gonna do is give Trig a call,' Dillon said decisively. 'Then we'll get Midge and Plank round and all get our heads together on this one.'

Ted felt better already, he knew Dillon would organise everything, rally the lads, make a plan. He was the sensible one of all of them, the 'leader', mostly because that was the role he'd been appointed from the age of twelve when his dad had walked out on his mum, their three sons and a daughter. His older brother Trig had had to go out and get a job to feed them all and Dillon had been left to help bring up his two younger siblings. Trig had ditched the job before long and found more lucrative methods of making money, all of which had landed him in trouble. He'd been in and out of jail since he was seventeen. Dillon had then had to move into the position of man-of-the-house, a job he'd done much better than his older brother. Trig now lived in a squat but came home every so often for a shower and a good feed, something his mum insisted on. Dillon knew he could always call on him if he needed anything, and if anyone knew how to manipulate the system it was Trig and his mates.

Mrs M waddled back in with a tray of steaming food as Dillon dialled the first number. 'Here you go, love,' she whispered to Ted as she placed a huge plate of bangers and mash topped with two fried eggs on his lap. 'This should get you started.' She winked. Ted beamed at her and winked back; a little flirting always guaranteed dessert. Mrs M giggled as she left the room. 'Leave room for afters,' she called behind her.

As they ate, Dillon organised the meet-up. Trig did most of his work at night, so Midge and Plank were coming to Dillon's to see Ted that night, and then Ted and Dillon would go over to Trig's the next day.

Ted sat back and patted his full stomach. Thanks to Dillon he felt hopeful for the first time, like maybe there was a chance they would be able to find Rosie, despite the sheer magnitude of London and all its workings.

Midge and Plank arrived half an hour later, a case of beer at the ready. Midge rarely did anything without the help of beer, or smokes for that matter. He threw his short tubby body at Ted when he saw him, his head only reaching to Ted's shoulders. Ted slapped him on the back and then rubbed his receding hairline. It had become a bit of a ritual to rub Midge's shiny big forehead like the genie's lamp, so they could make a wish, and Ted had a lot to wish for.

'Granted,' said Midge.

'Let's hope so, mate,' replied Ted.

Plank was the opposite of Midge; he was tall and lanky, with thick wild hair that stuck out at all angles. He was often called the mad professor, partly because of his hair but also because he was something of a genius. Plank rarely told many people that he could work for NASA if he wanted because he was embarrassed it was uncool, but the others were secretly jealous.

'Back already? Countryside full of shit, eh?' asked Plank.

It was like old times. They all sat around drinking beer and catching up on what had been happening with each other. Plank had met a girl, a friend of Molly's who was Ted's ex. Her name was Gwen and she was half Plank's height but he didn't care: he was in lust.

All Midge had done since he'd last seen Ted was complete Dragon Age, and get his fastest time yet on Grand Theft Auto IV.

Then it was Ted's turn and they all listened to him tell the story again. When he'd finished there was silence as each of them digested what they'd been told. Plank spoke first.

'I hate to be the one to state the obvious, but how do we even know she's still in London?'

Ted ran his hand through his messy dark hair and sighed. 'We don't, I just don't have any other leads.'

'Well it's as good a place as any to start,' said Midge. 'Even if she was here but isn't anymore we may still be able to get on her trail. Bloody bastards. Any idea what they may want with her?'

'I try not to let my head go there, Midge,' replied Ted quietly.

'But there's been no ransom demand or anything?'

'No, not that I've heard. They wouldn't get much out of ransoming her anyway, we're broke!'

Ted got up and started pacing. There wasn't much space between the two chairs and sofa that filled the tiny living room; there was only a narrow strip between the backs of the chairs and the front door that lent itself to any decent pacing action. The others swung round to face him, their heads moving back and forth as if they were watching a slow-motion game of tennis.

'Clever of her to leave the drawing of the lighter,' said Plank. 'I'd never even noticed it on The Streets album covers before.'

'That's coz you like Beethoven and Bach!' goaded Midge.

'Only when I'm working. It's soothing,' defended Plank, his face filling with embarrassment.

'It was clever of her, but it only gets us this far,' said Ted. 'I just don't know what to do next. I do know that time is running out, though. Whatever we do it has to be soon, she could be suffering right now whilst we're sitting here and talking about it.'

'We understand, mate, really, but we can't just roam the streets in the hope of seeing her. Trig will have some ideas, he knows people,' said Dillon quietly, glancing towards the kitchen.

'What about the cops, what are they doing?' asked Plank.

'Who knows,' replied Ted. 'They'll do all the routine stuff, I guess, but they probably won't have any idea where to start looking in London either.'

Ted followed Dillon's look at the kitchen door. 'Does she know why I'm here?' he asked.

'No, I wasn't sure if you wanted anyone else to know,' replied Dillon.

'Well I guess the more people that know the more eyes there will be to spot her,' said Ted, still pacing. 'You think she knows anything that might help us?'

'It's worth asking, I guess; you never know with my mum.'

Ted was so tired of telling the story of his moment of weakness, and he wasn't sure if he wanted Dillon's mum to know what a hopeless brother he was. She held him in such high regard that he didn't want to disappoint her. He could feel his friends' eyes boring into him, awaiting a reaction, a decision, something, and realised he'd stopped pacing and was staring at the kitchen door. He shook his head as if that would help rid him of the confusion that had made a home there. He turned to Dillon.

'Do you think you could tell her? I can't go through it all again today.'

'Sure, I'll go see her now,' Dillon replied. He stood up and squeezed Ted's shoulder as he passed.

Ted slumped down in the chair Dillon had vacated. It was warm and comforting and he realised how tired he was. Plank and Midge looked around awkwardly and Ted realised they must feel as helpless as he did.

Ted's phone rang and he jumped on it.

'Ted?' said the voice. For a brief second Ted's heart leapt, it sounded so like Rosie; but then their voices were very similar.

'Hey, Mum,' he said, quietly.

'How you doing, darling? Did you get to Dillon's OK?'

'Yeah. We're just trying to work out what to do next. Any news from the cops?'

'Not yet. Your dad and I are coming up to London tomorrow. The police want us nearby, in case…' Her voice faded away.

'So they think she's probably in London too?' asked Ted hopefully.

'They think it's the most likely place at this time, although they're not sure how long she'll be there, whether whoever has her plans to take her elsewhere.'

'Do they have any idea who may have her or why?' Ted wasn't sure he wanted to hear the answer but he had to ask.

There was silence on the other end of the phone.

'Mum?'

Ted heard her sigh. 'They think there's a chance she may have got caught up with smugglers or traffickers of some kind. Somewhere like that bunker, right next to the sea, is a prime spot to bring goods in from the sea and then from there transport them north; to London most likely, at least initially.'

'You don't mean like pirates, surely? I thought Dad was only joking about them!'

'Not in the way he was describing them but yes, in a way. Except instead of treasure they bring in anything from weapons to drugs, even people.'

'People?'

'Apparently, yes, to sell or make money from in some other way…' She quietened.

'Sell them? How can you sell another human being?' Ted asked, incredulous. He couldn't believe what he was hearing.

'I don't know, darling,' she whispered.

'But what do they sell them for?'

Ted heard his mum sob and then a rustling. 'Ted, it's Dad. Your mum's a bit upset.'

'Hi, Dad.'

'Listen, the police were vague, obviously not wanting to worry us, but reading between the lines it seems that Rosie could be in danger of being sold for prostitution.'

Ted was shocked by his dad's bluntness, he was usually so optimistic and sought out the positive in everything, but his voice had a strange edge, like he was struggling to hold himself together. Ted couldn't speak; his throat had slammed shut at the word prostitution. His little sister… how could all this have happened so fast, and to them? Things like this always happened to other people; nameless, faceless people in the news. People who probably deserved it, who weren't careful, who took their lives for granted, who didn't pay attention to the world around them and take responsibility for it, people who left it all for someone else to deal with – other people, not them.

'Ted, are you there?'

'I'm here, Dad.'

'I'm sorry to be so blunt but there's no point sugar-coating it for you.'

'I know, Dad, and I appreciate it.'

'Listen, better go and get organised, just wanted to tell you what was going on this end. Be safe and keep in touch, OK?'

'Sure. Bye, Dad.'

'Your mum sends her love. Bye, Ted.'

Ted told the others what his mum and dad had said. Dillon sat down when Ted had finished; he looked older than Ted remembered.

'It's funny, my mum just said the same thing. I was hoping it was just her overactive imagination but maybe not.'

'What made her think it might be people traffickers though?' asked Ted.

'Well partly because she watches a lot of TV, and partly because her cousin's daughter was trafficked.'

Ted rested his head in his hands. One minute he knows nothing about trafficking, and the next he knows someone who knows someone who was trafficked, as well as possibly his own sister.

'It's like when you buy something you've never had before,' said Ted, looking up through blurred, red eyes, 'like a different phone or car; you suddenly realise how many others have the same as you, but before you got yours you'd never noticed.'

'Eh?' Dillon looked puzzled.

'Well I never even noticed or paid any attention to trafficking because it had never happened to me or anyone I knew, but now that it has happened to someone I know, it seems like it's everywhere!'

'That's so true!' piped up Plank. 'I had no idea about asthma until my sister had it and now I see people puffing on their inhalers all the time. Funny how that works; like you're blind to everything until it enters your peripheral vision, despite the fact it's there all the time.'

'That's deep, man,' said Midge, nodding solemnly.

'Oh shut up you brainless, bald idiot!' spat Plank.

'Now, now, kids,' scolded Dillon.

'So what happened to your mum's cousin's daughter then?' asked Ted, fighting the desire to tell Midge to be serious for once.

As if on cue, Mrs M walked into the room. She seemed sadder than when Ted had seen her earlier as she forced a smile towards Plank and Midge. Ted rose and offered her his seat, which she gratefully accepted.

'I'm sorry to hear about Rosie,' she began. 'It's truly awful.'

'Thank you.' Ted smiled. 'Dill said your cousin experienced something similar with her daughter,' coaxed Ted, hungry for any information.

Mrs M lowered her eyes and tugged at a stray bit of cotton hanging from her shirt. She seemed unsure of what to say so Ted waited patiently for her to speak. Finally she took a deep breath and began.

'It was under very different circumstances that my cousin Angelica's daughter was trafficked. Where we're from, in

Nigeria, they do things very differently, in ways that are hard for Westerners to comprehend. Most Nigerians are very religious; their entire belief system revolves around God and doing his bidding – the Niger Delta, where we all lived, claims to have more churches per square mile than any other place on Earth; we had three within a mile of the house we grew up in. Anyway, there are people, so-called religious leaders, who take advantage of the strength of those beliefs and manipulate them to gain power over others.'

Mrs M stared into the empty fireplace like she was watching a scene play out in front of her. It was clearly an uncomfortable subject for her, as she seemed unable to meet anyone's eyes. Ted wondered if she was ashamed about what she was telling them.

'Another thing you need to understand about Nigeria is that there is a lot of poverty, disease and hunger, but also a lot of money. These two extremes exist side by side; the problem is that the rich can dip their filthy fingers into the poor side, but the poor aren't able to do the same in return. Having all that wealth under their noses makes the poor angry and jealous and they don't understand why they can't have some of the money. They search for someone or something to blame; they can't blame God because he is their salvation, so instead they blame the devil, or rather the devil's children – any child from a family that is poor or diseased is said to be the cause of the suffering and so is named a witch. And the religious leaders I mentioned earlier use this as their manipulation. They are the ones that encourage this absurd belief, because they can then offer a solution; namely exorcism, which can cost families up to a year's income. During the exorcism, or deliverance, the children are shaken violently and have "potions" poured into their eyes, all the while their parents watch and pray that it works because if it doesn't they know their children will be killed. Many children are held in churches, often on chains, and deprived of food until they "confess" to being a witch.'

Mrs M took an audible breath like she had wanted to get the story out as quickly as possible and had forgotten to breathe. Ted nodded encouragingly; afraid she would find it all too much and stop.

'The families who can't afford to pay to have their witch-child cleansed have to face the possibility of the child being banished from the community, or worse; burned, buried alive, sometimes poisoned or drowned, even hacked to death with machetes.'

As Mrs M wiped the tears from her eyes, Ted was now unsure he wanted to hear the rest.

'The point of this gruesome story is that there were men who would pay to take the child witches away, far away, to a better life abroad. Which is what Angelica chose for her daughter who was accused of being a witch. Angelica couldn't afford to have her exorcised and the community had already cut out her daughter's tongue and poured acid over her in an attempt to rid her of the devil themselves, so her only choice was to send her away.

'Angelica later found out that the men that had taken her daughter were traffickers, but by then it was too late.'

Mrs M blew her nose loudly, shattering the silence left in her story's wake. A whole new world had opened up like a gaping hole in front of Ted and he felt as if he was teetering on the edge of it, unable to pull himself back from the brink of its fiery depths.

'How is this allowed to happen?' he whispered, mostly to himself.

Mrs M looked at him through tear-filled eyes.

'No one cares, it's as simple as that. It's no one else's problem.'

'Has Angelica ever tried to find her daughter?' asked Plank.

'She has no means of doing that. I managed to get out of the country thanks to Dillon's father who was English and in Nigeria working in the oil fields for a while, but Angelica married a poor man and so had to stay there. I have tried looking for her daughter in London, just in case she was brought here, but there are so many other countries she could have been taken to,' said Mrs M sadly.

'How did you know where to look or who to ask?' said Ted desperately.

'Well, that's partly why I told you this long story. A friend of mine has a daughter that works behind the bar in a strip club in Soho. She told me there are girls coming and going all the time, many of whom have stories to tell, and tell them freely after a few drinks and drugs. I went there and asked some of them if they'd seen her, no one had but they had come across lots of foreign girls that had been trafficked. It's a place worth trying anyway.'

Ted got up from where he was sitting on the floor, a flicker of hope in his heart. 'Right, well it's a place to start,' he said firmly, smiling gratefully at Dillon's mum. She nodded and wrote down the name and address of the club.

Midge jumped up too.

'We'll come with you,' he said. 'I'm excellent at charming the ladies, I can always get them to talk.'

Despite the anguish Ted was feeling, he couldn't help cracking a smile. 'Lead the way then, double-o-seven!'

# Chapter 9

Rosie rocked back and forth, her knees pulled up under her chin, her eyes staring unblinking at the blank wall. Except that it wasn't the blank wall she was seeing, it was Lo's tiny face and pleading eyes, his little outstretched arms begging her for help. She had known him for such a short time and yet the guilt she felt for failing him was opening up a new hole in her chest. And the worst thing was she had no idea where he had been taken or whether he was coming back. London was a terrifying place even to someone who knew it as well as she did, but to a little boy who couldn't even speak the language it must be like a never-ending ride through the House of Horrors.

Baduwa came and sat down beside her. Rosie thought she could see a glimmer of sympathy in her pretty eyes, but maybe it was pity in the worst sense. Baduwa stroked her hair gently.

'I could make your hair look pretty if you like?' she offered. 'You could borrow my hair clip for a while, it'll make you feel better.'

Rosie felt like slapping her. 'Why would I want to look pretty?' Rosie snarled.

'So that you'll get picked next time,' said Baduwa, cocking her head on one side like a confused puppy.

Rosie sprang to her feet in fury. 'Why the hell would I want to be picked? Those people aren't kind like you think, they're monsters! They keep us locked in a tiny room, feed us pig slop, and pluck us out one by one like battery hens going to the slaughter.'

Baduwa rose in anger, her hands balled fists at her sides. 'You don't know that! He's going to come for me soon and you'll be left wishing it was you.'

Baduwa stomped to the other side of the room and curled up on one of the mattresses. Utibe stood in the middle looking from her to Rosie as if uncertain who to comfort. She chose Baduwa.

Rosie felt bad. She shouldn't have shouted at Baduwa like that, she should have just left her to her delusions. It must be comforting to be so unaware. Rosie was about to apologise when the door opened and Zaydain walked in. Rosie shrank back against the wall, wishing it would open up and swallow her. He flung some clothes in her direction and ordered her to put them on, then did the same to Utibe and Baduwa. Dropping a bag into the middle of the room he then told them to find a pair of shoes that fitted them.

'I'm not putting these on! You can't make me!' said Rosie, kicking the clothes away.

Zaydain walked towards her, his eyes piercing her soul, and grabbed her by the throat.

'You will put them on or I will hurt your family, it's as simple as that,' he said, spitting each word. His face was so close Rosie could see the tiny hairs above his lips breaking the surface of his skin. His breath smelt of cigarettes and evil. Rosie hardly breathed as he held her against the wall, his body pressing against hers. Then he let her go and she dropped to the floor.

Rosie held her neck where his hand had been, gulping back the vomit that had entered her mouth. Her family: she hadn't even thought they might get hurt.

Zaydain leant against the wall, his eyes impatient and disinterested as she slowly put on a small lace top with a bra sewn inside it, then a short skirt with a split up the side. There was also a brown wig cut in a short bob with a straight fringe. Brushing her own hair under the wig, she subconsciously pushed herself aside to make way for the other person she was now expected to be. She couldn't fight anymore, or even entertain the idea of escape, not if it meant her family might get hurt. She'd caused them enough pain.

Rosie stood, pulling sheepishly at the skirt in an attempt to make it longer. It didn't seem to want to oblige so she gave up and just shivered.

'Put these on,' ordered Zaydain, throwing coats to all of them. 'And brighten up your miserable mouths with this,' he said, tossing them each a lipstick.

Rosie's was called Orange Sunset and it smelt of her old history teacher who she would give anything to be with right now, despite her wonky eyes and bad breath.

Griff suddenly appeared in the doorway and they each slipped on a pair of shoes and were marched out into the cool night.

Rosie's shoes pinched her feet as she tottered along at the back. Baduwa stumbled ahead, desperately trying to master a confident, sexy walk, but her drooping shoulders and frightened, darting eyes gave her away, and Rosie realised that Baduwa was beginning to lose her beautiful plumage.

As they were bundled into the car, Zaydain cursed under his breath and ran back towards the building they had just left. Griff sat in the front seat shifting nervously. Rosie was alarmed to find she pitied him; he was like a child in every way except for his size, and she wondered whether he felt just as trapped and helpless as the rest of them. She looked up and caught his dark eyes watching her in the mirror; there was an unnerving yearning in them that made Rosie gasp and look away. Baduwa shot her a look but Rosie just shook her head.

'Put these on,' said Zaydain, getting back into the car and passing each of them a small drawstring bag.

Rosie opened hers tentatively, expecting a large spider to crawl out and bite her hand, but instead found a small key on a chain. She saw that the others had the same ornate keys, unlike any Rosie had seen before. Turning it over in her hand, Rosie thought how ironic it was that they had been given a key when they were anything but free.

'Put it on,' Zaydain ordered again.

'What's it for?' asked Rosie.

'Access all areas,' Zaydain sneered.

Rosie did as she was told and then sat back to gaze out of the window at the streaking lights, her flickering eyes desperately searching the passing shops and houses for a spark of recognition, a clue that she'd been there before. For ages there was nothing familiar and she began to fear that she'd somehow got it wrong and they weren't in London at all, but soon the buildings became denser and higher and Rosie suddenly saw a department store she'd visited many times with her mum. Her heart ached at the memory and tears rushed to her eyes. It was like seeing an old friend, and she felt homesick for her childhood and the relationship she used to have with her mum, before everything.

They turned down Regent Street, past more shops ornately decorated to tantalise the discerning shopper, then onto Piccadilly Circus with its unmistakeable light show. Despite how late it must have been, the city was still very much alive and pulsating with activity.

Rosie looked at Baduwa and Utibe, their transfixed faces illuminated by neon, and realised they would never have seen anything like this before; this place that Rosie had called home for so long was a wonderland full of possibilities to them. But through new eyes Rosie could see it was all just a mirage, a façade designed to fool anyone stupid enough to be hypnotised by the bright lights and promise of something better.

The car swung round the Circus and into Shaftesbury Avenue, the gateway to Soho. The neon lights reduced in size and the streets narrowed as they wound through them, the car finally pulling to a stop outside what looked like a nightclub. The imposing black sign read 'The Lock', and Rosie felt Baduwa stiffen next to her.

The three of them were ordered out of the car where they stood shivering on the pavement as Zaydain spoke to the man on the door. Then they were pushed inside. The sound of thumping music echoed from somewhere beneath them as they had their coats removed, and Rosie began to feel like a doll, a puppet, whose own actions were not required as she was pushed and pulled and directed all the way down into the depths of the club.

It was a large, cavernous space with balconies spiralling down over three floors and one vast dance floor at the centre. Lights flashed and streaked across the club, highlighting the happy faces of the hundreds of dancers pulsating in one huge mass, like a swarm of bees in a hive. As Rosie looked closer she saw that along the balconies were little pockets of seats from where the dance floor could be viewed, and each pocket was filled with men and women laughing together.

The girls were steered round the back of the balconies and along a corridor to where a large ornate curtain hung, guarded by two men. They nodded at Zaydain as he handed them a card and pointed to the keys around the girls' necks. The men stood aside to let them walk behind the curtain and through a door. Rosie almost felt like laughing, was this a joke? Surely things like this didn't really go on? The room was small and intimate, far removed from the rest of the club, with tables nestled in booths surrounding a much smaller dance floor where there were young boys and girls dancing together. Some looked awkward but others seemed to be really enjoying the attention from the people sitting at the tables, their hungry eyes focussed on the dancers.

'Time to earn your keep,' Zaydain hissed in Rosie's ear. 'Dance!'

Rosie looked at him in horror, but the warning in his eyes prompted her to move, slowly, awkwardly, unable to find her usual ease of rhythm. Baduwa and Utibe began to move too, never taking their startled eyes off their surroundings. Rosie noticed there were a few small podiums dotted around the dance floor and on each one was a huddle of girls dancing together, some shyly and some with gusto. As she looked closer she noticed, to her horror, that they were all wearing the same keys that she and Baduwa and Utibe were wearing. What did it all mean?

'Look sexy!' growled Zaydain.

Rosie had never looked sexy in her life and had no idea how, so she started moving her arms more vigorously, nodding her head in time to the beat. Baduwa knew how, though, and Rosie watched as she curled and spun around, stroking her body as she moved. She even began to look like she was enjoying herself as a small smile played on her lips. This was what she loved, after all, thought Rosie, to be the centre of attention and be admired like a beautiful bird. Maybe this was where Baduwa belonged; perhaps this was a million times better than the life she had left in Nigeria. Rosie tried to copy some of her moves, anything to stop Zaydain scowling at her.

Once he seemed satisfied that they were doing the best they could, Zaydain led them to a podium and helped each of them climb up. Rosie suddenly felt more self-conscious and tried to hide between Baduwa and Utibe, which, surprisingly, neither of them seemed to mind. Even Utibe was getting into the music. Rosie wished she could find enjoyment in their situation; it would make things so much easier, somehow.

She suddenly noticed that the lights were doing something to the keys around Baduwa and Utibe's neck; they were revealing a number that was written on them in some strange pen. She looked down at her own and the same was happening; the number on her key was 133. Rosie looked around them, trying to find answers in the crowd. As she did she noticed there were a lot of eyes on them, or rather on her. A red laser shone in her eyes and then onto her chest. She followed the beam back to a man sitting in one of the booths and saw him nod towards another man. Before she knew it, she was being dragged down from the podium and ushered over to the table. She glanced back at the terrified faces of Baduwa and Utibe as she was taken and placed in front of the man who had shone the light on her.

'Even better up close,' he sniffed, rubbing his moustache. 'This one's going to need special time and attention, I'll reserve her for another night,' he said to the man holding on to Rosie's arm. The man released her arm briefly and wrote something in a book. He nodded and then dragged Rosie away and placed her back on the podium.

Baduwa looked questioningly at her as she danced, but Rosie could only shrug. She couldn't bring herself to tell Baduwa what had happened or what she now realised was probably about to happen many times over to all of them.

# Chapter 10

The city still held the same excitement for Ted, despite the circumstances, and he felt confident as he strode through the streets of Soho, following the directions that Mrs M had given them. They passed one of their favourite bars and each of them looked longingly in the window, wishing they were there for the casual, carefree nights they used to have. So much seemed to have happened in just a few days that Ted could hardly remember what it felt like to have no worries, to take everything so for granted.

As they turned down the street leading to the nightclub, the hair on the back of Ted's neck bristled. It was darker than the other streets and dotted with shifty-looking men scurrying up and down it, popping out of doorways, blinking as their eyes adjusted to the bright flashing neon lights that promised GIRLS! GIRLS! GIRLS!

'Right, everyone,' said Ted, shaking off the fear. 'We've got to appear like we want to go into this place so lots of drunken shouting and leering, OK?'

'That should be no problem for you, Midge,' scoffed Plank.

'Funny,' retorted Midge. 'Maybe we should pretend it's your stag, Ted, then you might get special treatment.'

'That's not a bad idea, Midge,' said Dillon. 'You up for that, Ted?'

'Sure, let's do it.'

They all began laughing and shouting, staggering down the street and hanging off each other. They arrived outside the door of the club where Dillon did some quick talking to the bouncer and they were shown straight in and directed to a booth in front of a small stage. It was as Ted had expected; dark, seedy, full of barely-dressed girls, most of them not much older than Rosie. He didn't even recognise the music that was playing, it sounded like some Eastern European country's entry in Eurovision.

They were seated on a purple velvet sofa with dim lighting hanging low above their heads. The stage in front of them was alive with crawling, slithering pole-dancing girls, all selling their own brand of seduction. They ordered a drink each and found themselves closely administered to by four girls. Not that any of them really minded about this part of the detective work, though Ted couldn't help envisaging Rosie doing something similar, and that instinctively made him shy away from the exhaustive attention.

Ted excused himself and sought refuge in the gents. He had to pull himself together or the girls would never trust him enough to talk. Plank and Midge were having a great time and seemed very at home, but he'd seen the same look in Dillon's eyes that he felt were present in his own, and knew he was struggling too.

When Ted got back to the table there were more drinks and the girl who had been sitting with him previously had been replaced by another; obviously they had misinterpreted his distaste and swapped her for another girl. Unfortunately this one reminded him even more of Rosie, innocence still obvious in her eyes, so Ted took a deep breath as he put his arm around her, slugging back his beer, forcing the vision of his sister to the back of his mind to deal with later. He caught eyes with Dillon who seemed to be having the same grim thoughts about his own sister and was swigging liberally on his beer too, quickly chasing it with a vodka.

'So what's your name?' Ted asked the girl.

'What do you want it to be?'

Ted rolled his eyes. 'You're joking, right?'

'I am here to give you pleasure,' she replied. 'You can call me what you like.'

'Well, I'm Ted,' he said. 'Where are you from?' he asked, trying to place her accent.

'An island in Croatia called Vis.'

'Your English is very good. Have you been in the UK for long?'

'A while, but I talk to many English men and not so hard to pick up the talk.'

'A lot of them like to talk, do they?' Ted asked, surprised.

'Yes. Lots of them just want someone to talk to. Well, in the start.'

'How old are you?' As the question came out of his mouth and her eyes flicked away, Ted realised he'd lost her.

'I'm sorry, that's none of my business,' he said hurriedly.

She shrugged and leaned over, sticking her tongue in his ear. 'You like me to dance for you?'

Ted looked across at the others, each enjoying a lap dance of their own. Despite their drunken grins of pleasure it didn't encourage him to want one too, and he shook his head.

'Look, I'm sorry, actually, I need some help, do you think you could help me?' Ted rushed, feeling the pressure of time again and realising that a moment of pleasure for him here could mean a moment of horror for Rosie somewhere else. The girl looked confused, then her expression changed to that of understanding and she nodded, taking his hand and leading him into another, more private room. It was quieter and clearly reserved for more intimate dances. As soon as she had shut the door she began undressing him.

'I can help you with anything you like,' she whispered in his ear.

'No, no!' Ted blurted out, pushing her away roughly. 'Not that kind of help!'

The girl looked frightened as she cowered in the corner, hurriedly doing up her dress.

'Look, I'm sorry.' Ted sighed, holding up his hands. 'It's nothing to do with you. I am trying to find my sister and I need help. That's what I meant.'

The girl didn't move for a moment but must have read the pleading in Ted's eyes because she tentatively sat down on the sofa awaiting an explanation.

Ted began the story he felt he'd told a million times already. When he'd finished, he said, 'I realise it's nothing to do with you, and you have absolutely no obligation to help me, but if you know anything that may help me find her I'd be so grateful.' He rummaged in his wallet and waved some notes in her direction.

Ted stared desperately into her eyes, feeling utterly vulnerable as he realised this was his only lead, and if she couldn't help him he was back to nowhere. He doubted the others had been able to keep to the task in hand, not when there were other, far greater temptations, so it all hung on what came out of her mouth next. Ted was aware he was leaning right into her face and he checked himself, giving her room.

Her eyes were sad as she looked up at him; they showed no signs of surprise, merely resignation as if she'd heard it all before. Ted suddenly remembered the photo of Rosie and pulled it out of his wallet to show the girl.

'She's beautiful... but I can't help you. I know nothing about this trafficking you say. Sorry, you have to go. If I don't work I get trouble.'

Ted noticed her glance at the large mirror on the wall for the third time since they'd entered the room. He forced a smile and thanked her as they went to join the others.

Dillon looked at him questioningly as he returned but Ted merely shook his head. He felt burning panic as he realised that it was going to be impossible to find Rosie in this world, they were all too secretive, like an exclusive club that most of them probably didn't want to belong to but couldn't be allowed to leave.

Ted looked around him at the other men crawling with girls, their eyes moist pools of pleasure, their mouths fixed in a half-smile that even in itself seemed to take more effort than they would like, as they sat slumped in their seats with their hands groping and squeezing whatever they could reach. Ted hated them all for their blatant lack of control, for fuelling the fire that was already burning way out of control. He was even starting to resent being a man himself.

He leaned across to Dillon and told him he was leaving. Dillon immediately nodded to say he was coming too. Midge and Plank, however, looked like they were far too engrossed to pull themselves away, so Ted just said he'd see them tomorrow and headed for the exit. As he was leaving someone grabbed his hand and pushed something into it. He turned and saw the Croatian girl; she didn't look at him as she walked past and entered the toilet.

Ted waited until they got outside to look in his hand. It was a piece of paper, and on it was written just two words: The Lock.

Dillon looked at Ted. 'I saw that name on the way here. It's just a few streets away.'

They started running, hope daring to flicker to life in Ted's heart. They had no idea what they would find at The Lock but the fact that the girl had given them a lead meant they had something to do, somewhere to go.

They wound in and out of streets, some dark and sinister, some still bustling with life; Ted marvelled at the city that never slept. Eventually they reached the sign that Dillon remembered seeing. It wasn't bright and flashing like the others but written in black letters against a wooden background. It wasn't shouting about its existence but it was there in bold if you knew what you were looking for. They marched up to the door, unsure of the response they'd get, but the bouncer stood aside to let them in. Ted and Dillon looked at each other. Could it really be so easy? Were they going to find Rosie and get to go home?

They walked down the steps, following the sound of the beat. Ted felt positive suddenly, and found himself moving to the music. It wasn't the kind of place they normally went to: the lights were too bright and the music too jumpy, but it was quite a spectacular place to behold.

'I think I've read about this place,' said Dillon suddenly. 'Isn't this the club owned by that football manager? Umm, can't think of his name. Anyway, it's meant to be the largest in Europe or something, and reaches further underground than any other club,' he said, tapping his forehead like he was trying to dislodge the memory.

'Dunno, mate, I've never heard of it. Looks impressive though.'

They bought a beer each and stood leaning over the balcony, watching the dancing below. Girls caught their eyes and beckoned to the boys to join them on the dance floor.

'How are we gonna play this one?' asked Dillon. 'Are we just looking or should we be asking around?'

'Let's look first,' said Ted. He didn't want to alert anyone to their presence just yet. They were a jumpy bunch, and Ted was beginning to realise it was going to take something more subtle than direct questioning.

Dillon nodded and took the lead down the stairs. They tried to look casual as they wandered in and out of dancers and then past the booths, but no one seemed to pay them any attention. They could see no sign of anything dodgy; there were some young girls but they seemed to be there of their own free will and it wasn't unusual to see underage girls at clubs.

They went back up the stairs to the second floor and walked along the balconies. More people lounged in booths, their tables laden with a myriad of empty glasses. Ted noticed that each booth had its own bar; there were drinks dispensers fitted into a mini bar at the back where you could put your glass and fill it up with anything you desired. Like an alcohol vending machine, thought Ted in awe, and suddenly he longed to have a go.

Ted felt a pull on his arm and Dillon hissed in his ear that he was gawping. Ted hurried along behind Dillon and up to the top floor. More of the same, and still nothing that gave them any idea what the girl had meant by sending them to this bar. Ted began to feel desperate again and wondered if they should ask around.

'This doesn't make sense,' he said. 'You think she was just trying to get us out of the way?'

'I dunno, mate. Perhaps we should go, just for now. I'll speak to Trig, get him to find out the insiders on this place. Then when we know more we can come back.' Dillon patted Ted on the shoulder and indicated towards the door. Ted took one last look around and followed him out.

They walked away from The Lock, the sign diminishing in the distance like Ted's fragile hopes. Ted suddenly slumped down on the kerb in defeat, his head finding a familiar place in his hands.

'I'll call Trig,' said Dillon, sitting down beside Ted. 'He might be able to ask around about the club before we see him tomorrow.'

Ted nodded and looked back at The Lock in the distance; it seemed like such an insignificant place from the outside, and there had been no sign of anything sinister inside. What had that girl meant them to find? Just then a car pulled up outside. The door of the club swung open releasing the deep drone of the music inside, and a man walked out, followed by three girls in long coats. Two of them looked black, and the other, with short brown hair, was white. They were all pushed hurriedly into the car before it sped along the road towards Ted and Dillon, narrowly missing their feet.

# Chapter 11

Rosie lay curled in a tight ball on the filthy mattress, dawn breaking outside the window, the birds gloating as they sang about the start of a new day and how great it was to be free. She was exhausted but couldn't clear her mind of all the men that had leered at her, studied her; 'booked' her for another day. Only Baduwa had been what they'd called 'engaged' that night. Not that she would talk about it. She had been taken off, the same as Rosie, although she was gone for longer, and when she returned her face spoke of the horror of what had happened to her. All Rosie and the others could do was hold her tightly in their arms in the hope that they could replace some of what she had lost.

Rosie knew it was merely a matter of time until it was her turn. She could only imagine what awaited her. Her stomach churned and twisted with every vicious image, cold sweat rushed her with every terrifying thought that tried to creep into her mind. Her curled, shaking body fought the desire to rage and scream and panic, to tear at the windows, not caring if she ripped her arms to shreds. But how could she? Not when he'd threatened her family. Knowing they were safe was what kept her going; picturing them together, probably sad but at least together was reassuring and the only thought that put up any fight against the others pushing their way uninvited into her head.

Rosie could hear Baduwa sobbing nearby as she relived her own horror and knew that soon she herself would be on the other side of what she knew now, like Baduwa, devoid of any remaining innocence.

Rosie wasn't sure if she'd slept when the door opened and food was dumped on the floor, but she suddenly realised how hungry she was and scrambled to the tray with the other two. She found herself being less fussy this time, not knowing where or when the next meal would appear. She forced down the lumpy porridge, chasing each mouthful with a gulp of milk. There was also toast smothered with margarine that she devoured hungrily. Rosie couldn't remember eating with such urgency before, like she was trying to fill the gaping void in her stomach. Baduwa and Utibe seemed to be doing the same, although they had eaten like this at their last meal so the hole in their stomachs must have been there longer.

After the brief distraction that eating brought, Rosie crawled back to her mattress to await the inevitable, and it wasn't long before someone entered the room. Rosie squeezed her eyes shut praying that they would take one of the others, not her, but then the door clicked shut and she slowly lifted her head off the mattress. Just inside the door were three towels and some soap. The relief was overpowering but so was the guilt that she'd wished the others would suffer in her place.

The shower didn't look like it had been cleaned in a while but the water ran hot which was all Rosie cared about as she stood under its reassuring stream hoping ashamedly that all her selfish thoughts were being washed away down the drain, down into the sewer with the rats where they belonged.

When Rosie had finished her shower she walked back into the room to find Lo sitting on her mattress, knees up under his chin. Rosie ran to him and pulled him close, but he was different somehow, more rigid, so she let him go, searching the eyes that wouldn't meet hers. A bruise was forming on his neck and she touched it gently, tears running down her cheeks, but he flinched away and lay down. Rosie had no words, not that he'd understand anyway, so she lay down next to him and pulled his little body close. Sleep felt like the best place for everyone right now.

***

It felt like no time at all before the opening door woke them. Lo immediately jumped up and ran to the furthest side of the room. But they weren't there for him. It was Rusty this time, and his face was positively aglow with excitement as he threw some clothes at Rosie and told her she had ten minutes to make herself look hot. Rosie scowled at him and blatantly waited until he had left the room. Despite his assurance that he'd seen it all before, there was no way she was letting him watch. The clothes were similar to the ones she'd worn the night before but slightly less revealing, smarter, like she was going somewhere respectable, which she doubted. Baduwa came and helped her put the wig on straight. She gave Rosie a hug and held her tight for a while.

'Just be somewhere else when it happens. Find a good memory and go there,' she whispered. Rosie nodded and pulled away just as the door opened and Rusty's smirk appeared.

'Ready? Ooo, yes you are! Not bad.'

Rosie put on the coat and turned to look at Lo and the girls once more. She managed a smile before following Rusty out of the door.

Rosie felt numb, empty. Whatever fear she had felt earlier was now gone, perhaps washed down the drain with the rest of her; whatever, she now felt a kind of acceptance that enabled her to put one foot in front of the other and walk. The journey was a haze of grey. She had no idea how long it took to get to the large house they pulled up outside. Time seemed to have lost all meaning, like in a dream, as Rosie was ushered in through the wooden doors and into a large reception room where there were four men playing snooker and swigging from beer bottles. They were old; forties, Rosie thought, a similar age to her dad.

Zaydain marched up to one and shook his hand. They went into another room, leaving Rosie to stand awkwardly in front of the other men. They began to move closer, like a pack of hyenas stalking their prey, laughter rippling from their lips in bursts of excitement as they nudged and coaxed each other to get even closer and perhaps touch her. Rosie cowered against the wall, leaning away from the stench of alcohol on their breath.

Zaydain entered the room again and they shrank back like they'd been caught trying to poach the lion's kill. For the first time Rosie felt grateful for Zaydain's presence and wished he wouldn't leave her. Maybe if she begged him to stay he would take pity on her. She suddenly felt her legs run out of the room and her hands battle with the lock on the front door to get outside, but Zaydain was right behind her and grabbed her round the waist.

'Please, please, I can't stay here. Take me back with you. I'll do anything you want, I'll do anything for you, I just can't…' Rosie broke down and her legs gave way. Zaydain held her up and dragged her to a chair in the corner.

'This isn't negotiable,' he hissed. 'These people have paid for you. You have to earn your keep, I'm not running a charity.'

Rosie looked up through her tear-filled eyes into his cold blue ones.

'I can get you the money if that's what you want. Please, they'll hurt me.'

Zaydain dragged her off the chair.

'You were so interested in what was going on when it had nothing to do with you, but now it does, you want out? Well, it doesn't work like that, you wanted in, so you're in.'

'Please… don't.' Rosie sobbed again.

Zaydain's face was set in a stone-like grimace as he dragged her back into the room.

'You have three hours. No marks,' he told the men.

Laughter trickled around the expectant group. 'Sure, we'll treat her like the princess she is.'

Rosie heard the front door slam behind Zaydain and knew she was really alone now. And as the men slowly advanced in her direction, their mouths askew with desire, Rosie remembered what Baduwa had said: find a good memory and go there. So she went on holiday to Cornwall with her family and thought about the sandcastles and ice creams, the games of frisbee, and eating fish and chips on the beach; not caring about the extra crunch of misplaced sand, because this was how life was meant to be. It was so bright and shiny everywhere in contrast to something dark that hung in her periphery: faces, hands, lips, teeth, heavy, hurt, a nightmare that never quite materialised into anything more than waves crashing on the shore and black storm clouds billowing on the horizon.

# Chapter 12

Dillon pulled back the corrugated iron sheet that covered the entrance to a courtyard. On it was painted *Danger. Condemned Building.* The courtyard led into a run-down conservatory and then through a front door into what Ted thought must have been an impressive house many years ago. Now it had leaks and holes and paint peeling off the walls, but the sweeping staircase and high ceilings told of a much more sophisticated past.

They heard barking coming from somewhere in the bowels of the house.

'Brace yourself,' said Dillon.

Ted looked at him questioningly but he didn't have to wait long for an answer as two vast dogs came skidding around the corner. Their legs scrabbled and scrambled as they tried to get a grip on the slippery floor and leap at them with their terrifying teeth bared.

'Scud! Missile! Down!' came a booming voice from somewhere in the house. To Ted's relief the dogs immediately sat down and started whimpering.

'That doesn't always happen.' Dillon grinned, looking rather relieved. 'Sometimes they knock you over before he says "down". Trig has to have his little amusements. He must be feeling kind today.'

They crept carefully past the dogs, catching a strong smell of weed wafting through the corridors.

Dillon smiled. 'This way.'

They followed the scent, passing many rooms, the smell growing stronger with every step. At last they came to a large room, empty except for one old sofa, a scattering of cushions and beanbags, and a plastic garden table with a chair where Trig was sitting at a computer, busily banging away at the keys.

'Boys,' he said as they entered.

'Hope we're not interrupting some private girl time there, Trig,' joked Dillon.

'No, I save the ladies for after dark, bruv. This is work. 'Ave a seat, I'll be with you in a minute.'

He tapped away some more and then shut the lid of the laptop, sitting back and folding his arms across his chest.

'So, I hear your sister's in a bit of bovver,' he said, looking at Ted.

Ted cowered under Trig's intimidating stare. It wasn't that he was a big bloke – on the contrary, he was shorter than both he and Dillon – but he had a presence about him, an air of authority. Ted figured it was from his time in prison and having to fend for himself. Plus he had a gang that he was the revered leader of. No one messed with Trig.

'Yeah,' said Ted, not knowing what else to say.

'Sit down, sit down,' said Trig, indicating to the many cushions scattered on the floor. They both did as they were told. 'Wanna beer?'

'Bit early for me, thanks,' said Dillon. Ted shook his head too.

'Suit yourselves,' said Trig, helping himself to one from the cool box next to the table. 'Kitchen's too far away to go all the way to the fridge.' He grinned.

'Did you manage to find anything out about that place, The Lock?' asked Dillon.

'As a matter of fact, I did,' replied Trig, looking pleased with himself. 'Right dodgy place by the sounds of it.'

Ted was confused. 'We were there last night and there was nothing dodgy going on.'

'But were you in the *right* place? See, there's the main club that the world gets to see, a flash and famous joint where loadsa celebs go, but behind that is something else: a members-only club where punters can view girls and boys, without interruption, in the comfort of the place. There is no age limit on what might be on display and you can pretty much order them for whatever you want, for how long you want.'

Ted felt bile rising in his throat. 'I will have one of those beers actually,' he said, getting up and walking over to the cool box.

'We never saw anything like that when we were there last night,' said Dillon.

'Of course not, this is not a place they want just anyone to know about,' scoffed Trig.

'Did you know there were places like this?' Dillon asked Trig. 'I knew there were some sick muckers out there but this seems so organised, so premeditated. Someone's put a lot of thought and money into this.'

'There was talk in prison, ya know, some of the real sick inmates boasted about shit they were into and where they could get it. But I had to dig quite deep to find out about The Lock. Seems it's protected by some very upper crust, influential people, if yer know what I mean. People that don't want to be recognised, and want somewhere anonymous to satisfy their sick fantasies.'

Ted gulped desperately at his beer, wishing it were something stronger.

'It's a massive club set over three floors with bangin' tunes. If it wasn't hell on earth it would be a wicked club to go to,' snorted Trig. 'Shame really.'

'So can we get in there?' said Ted, looking anxiously from Trig to Dillon.

'*We* can't, no…' said Trig.

Just then a door slammed somewhere in the house. The dogs barked. Trig shouted. There were footsteps coming closer and closer, then a bunch of people appeared in the doorway.

'…but *they* can,' finished Trig.

Ted looked at the motley collection of people standing in the doorway. There was a young woman and two men with what looked like a beaten drunk hanging off them. The woman strode over to Trig and sat on his knee, planting a long kiss on his mouth. The men dropped the drunk on the floor and went and helped themselves to a beer.

'Nice work. Is this 'im?' asked Trig, nodding towards the man on the floor.

The bottles hissed as the tops were flicked off.

'Yeah, this is William Hungerford,' said one of the men who towered above everyone. 'Where are your manners?' he shouted, walking over and kicking the body with a long leg. Ted could see why someone as small as Trig would have someone that huge around. 'Say howdie-do to everyone!' The body didn't move. 'Out cold.' He sniffed.

'Easy, Bill.' Trig laughed. 'Don't freak out our guests. You know my little brother Dill, and this is Ted whose sister we're trying to find.'

'Alright,' grunted Bill, slumping down on a cushion and slugging from his beer.

'That there is Dave,' continued Trig, nodding towards the smaller man who was busy rolling a joint. 'And this beauty is Blue,' he said, stroking her thigh.

Blue walked over to Dillon and kissed him on the cheek.

'Mmm, getting cuter by the day, Dill. You might have to be my replacement when your brother gets too old and incapable.' She grinned in Trig's direction.

'That'll never happen, baby,' said Trig, seemingly unperturbed by Blue's flirtation.

'What's going on, Trig?' asked Dillon, looking at the man on the floor.

'Oh yeah, sorry, you're probably wondering what the hell a half dead man is doing in my house!'

Dave grunted like a pig as he sat rolling a joint. Ted assumed he was laughing but couldn't be sure.

Trig walked over to the man on the floor and pulled open his jacket and shirt. He undid something from around his neck and dangled it from his hand. It was a key.

'William has been very helpful with our enquiries,' said Trig. 'Isn't that right, boys? Tell Ted and Dillon here what this key represents, my darlin',' he said, looking at Blue.

Blue stood up and took off her coat, clearly relishing her moment. 'Well,' she purred, holding the key seductively in her hand like a shopping channel presenter. 'This beautiful key will get you into The Lock, BUT only as William Hungerford. Each key has a number that can only be seen under a black light. This number corresponds with William's membership number. Therefore no one can steal the key and get in using it.'

She took the key from Trig and handed it to Ted. He turned it over in his hand. It was unlike any key he'd seen before; it was very ornate, old looking, like a key to an ancient tomb or something.

'Has William agreed to help us then? To get us in?' asked Ted.

They all laughed and Ted felt stupid.

'No, darlin',' soothed Blue. 'Not exactly.' She walked over and sat back on Trig's knee. 'Can I tell 'im?' she asked.

'Sure, babe, you did all the hard work,' replied Trig.

'Well,' she said, standing again. 'I have a sister who is a make-up artist for films and theatre 'n' that. She is going to make you up to look like William, Ted, so you can get into the club.' Blue did a twirl in the middle of the room, clearly pleased with herself.

Ted looked at the man on the floor; he was a similar build but was balding and older by about thirty years.

Blue saw his expression and smiled. 'My sister's very good at what she does. The body won't be a problem; she'll just have to work on your face and hair. The club have his details and photograph on a computer that they match to the number on the key, which we have, and your face, which we're going to change. There's no retinal scan or anything so high-tech. So we're sorted.' Blue twirled again, her long hair fanning out behind her. Ted was transfixed; everyone was. Except Dave, who was lying wasted on the floor, giggling and snorting like an idiot.

Ted felt overwhelmed. He'd never imagined Trig would manage to do so much in such a short time, and all for his sister. Although he wasn't sure he was a good enough actor to pull this off.

'Thank you,' was all Ted could say.

'No worries, mate. Any friend of Dillon's… Well, except for that prat you used to be friends with, Dill, what was his name? Radish or something?'

'Ravvy,' replied Dillon, 'and he wasn't that bad.'

'He was a complete plonker,' scoffed Trig.

'So when is all this going to happen?' asked Ted, suddenly feeling nervous.

'No time like the present, eh? It'll have to be tonight, someone might miss this loser if we hang on to him for too long. Although I can't think who,' scoffed Trig.

'But what if Rosie's not there tonight?' asked Dillon. 'If she even gets taken there, which we don't know, how will we know what night she goes?'

The room fell silent.

'That's a mighty good point, little bruv. Well maybe we'll have to keep William for a bit longer.' Trig paused, rubbing his chin. 'Bill, try and get a picture of one of William's kids, we'll have to use that to keep him quiet. And when he wakes up, 'ave 'im call his wife and tell her he's had to go on a last-minute business trip or something. That should buy us a few days. Will that be enough for you, Ted?'

Ted nodded slowly, unsure how long would be enough.

Blue clapped her hands with glee. 'We should have been coppers!' she squeaked.

'Nah,' said Trig. 'Too corrupt.'

Just then Ted's phone rang.

'Ted, it's mum,' came a quiet voice at the other end.

'Hi, how's things?' Ted asked, standing and walking out into the corridor.

'We're in London now. We just wanted to let you know, in case you need us for anything. We're feeling at rather a loose end. A bit helpless.'

'Any word from the police?'

'They keep us posted with what they're doing but they have no leads. She's just one of many children that go missing every day.' Her voice was an almost inaudible whisper and Ted had to strain to hear her. Ted so wanted to ease her pain by telling her what he was doing but he wasn't sure they would approve, and they would definitely insist he told the police and he knew that if this whole thing went as high as Trig had said, the police would be no help at all.

'I'm doing all I can, Mum. I'll let you know as soon as I hear anything,' he lied. 'Try not to worry.'

'Well, your dad and I are going to look anyway. We'll take a picture of her and ask around, all day and all night if we have to. We can't sit around waiting.'

'I know, Mum. Good luck and I'll come by and see you really soon, OK?'

'Bye, darling. We love you.'

Ted hung up the phone and stood staring down the corridor; a long tunnel that narrowed and darkened as it went away from him. He wished he could see a light at the end of it.

He only had a few days. What if she didn't show?

# Chapter 13

'Four big men like you had to tie a tiny defenceless girl up! Was she too much for you?' shouted someone nearby.

Rosie tried to move.

'What's wrong with you? You can pay extra for these bruises. No one else will want her looking like this. I'll have to cancel other clients!'

Rosie felt pulling on her arms and feet.

'She started off taking it like a lamb and then she went wild, biting and scratching. Look at my face, what will I tell my wife?'

'I don't give a fuck what you tell her!'

'I might need a tetanus shot. I didn't pay for that!'

Rosie tried to open her eyes as she was pulled to her feet. They hurt, as did her whole body. She stood, wobbling, squinting at the men around her. The room was a mess, and they all looked thoroughly wasted.

Zaydain made a call on his phone and soon Griff was carrying Rosie out to the car, her body screaming in agony with every step. As Griff poured Rosie gently in through the car door, she tried to pull herself upright in the seat so that she could at least see out of the window, her head held high. Griff shot her an occasional nervous glance, silent as always.

'Do you have any water?' Rosie asked tentatively.

Griff rummaged around on the floor by his feet and pulled out a bottle of water. The coolness soothed her sore mouth as Rosie drank desperately, wanting so badly to remember what had happened but unable to find anything in the blackness behind her eyes. There was something familiar about the confusion and heaviness she was feeling, though. Had she been drugged?

Zaydain swung himself into the driver's seat, looking back at Rosie briefly before saying something loudly in German; the only word Rosie recognising in the tirade of aggression was Gabriel. As the car swung around corners and screeched away from junctions, Rosie gripped the door handle to stop herself being thrown around, wincing at every thrust and jerk, unsure her damaged body could take any more abuse.

At last they reached the flat and as the door was closed behind her the expressions on the faces of Baduwa, Utibe and Lo told her that she looked as bad as she felt. Gathering around her they huddled together in mutual grief for all they had lost. Rosie sought out her family's faces in her mind, taking comfort in their smiles, afraid she would forget what they looked like when they were all she had to give her hope.

They must have fallen asleep in each other's arms because Rosie awoke to bright sunlight streaming through the window and her body aching as she tried to move. Lo grunted and turned away from her as she got slowly to her feet and limped to the bathroom shutting the door quietly behind her. She sat on the toilet seat, relieved there was no mirror to reveal the true horror of what went before, but as she lifted her skirt, her thigh turning purple then red like a sunset, all she could think about was how the only person who could make this all go away was her mum.

Suddenly there was a knock at the door and as Rosie quickly wiped the tears from her eyes, Baduwa peeped her head around the door.

'Are you OK? You've been in here for a while and I could hear you crying.'

Rosie nodded, but she wasn't OK, and she suspected Baduwa knew it.

Baduwa tore off some toilet paper and ran it under the cold tap. As she gently soothed Rosie's burning bruises with its coolness she whispered, 'I think my father sold me.'

Rosie looked up through aching eyes. The ringing in her ears was distorting Baduwa's voice; it sounded like she was on the other side of some thick glass.

'I've been thinking about it a lot ever since things turned out not to be how they had first seemed, and it's the only explanation. You remember I told you I met a man in Nigeria who offered to bring me here and promised me a house and a job and money?'

Rosie nodded, finally catching up with what Baduwa was talking about.

'Well I recognised him a little bit but I couldn't remember where I'd seen him before. But then I remembered last night. He was the friend of a man who worked for my dad. I'd seen him once at church and he'd stared at me the whole way through the service and made me nervous. Dad definitely knew him because they greeted each other like brothers.

Anyway, it was a few months after that he started hanging around and promising me the world.'

Baduwa paused to run some more paper under the tap.

'Dad talked me into it. I didn't even want to leave home but he said if I didn't I was making more work for my mum who already had three daughters to look after. I really miss my mum,' she whispered, squeezing out the paper and turning her attention to another bruise that Rosie hadn't noticed on her arm.

Rosie put her free hand on Baduwa's shoulder. 'Me too,' she whispered back.

'She didn't want me to leave, I know she didn't. She kept crying and telling me I didn't have to go, but I wanted to please my father and I didn't want to be a burden. And really I was quite excited. It was a chance to make a difference, to be special and beautiful. And I thought I could make a nice home and then they could all come and live with me here. But that's never going to happen, is it? I'm going to live like this for the rest of my life and never see my mama again.' She sobbed into Rosie's shoulder as Rosie held her tightly.

'We'll get out of here, we will,' promised Rosie with renewed determination. And in that moment she resolved to find a way to get them *all* out, whatever it took. It wasn't just her anymore, there were four of them, and each deserved their freedom.

When they walked back into the bedroom they found a tray of food. They ate in silence, Rosie hardly flinching at the quality of the food this time, as hunger became a blissful distraction from all other feelings.

Not long after they had finished, the door opened and Zaydain walked in. He threw clothes down in front of Utibe and Baduwa then walked out again without even looking at Rosie. Utibe and Baduwa stared at the clothes, aware by now what they meant, although Utibe had yet to be engaged by anyone. Despite the feeling of relief that she wasn't going this time, Rosie knew they were all suffering at the hands of the same enemy and it felt wrong, almost weak, to be letting them face it alone.

'Let's get this over with,' said Baduwa resignedly, pulling on the skirt. Utibe still seemed unsure of what was going on; merely copying everything Baduwa did as they changed in silence. Rosie helped them do up buttons and tidy hair. She gently fastened Baduwa's colourful clip, knowing that looking the best she could, whatever the situation, really mattered to her. Baduwa's hazel eyes met Rosie's and suddenly they were speaking a thousand words between them without opening their mouths. Rosie flung her arms around Baduwa and pulled Utibe close too.

'Remember, find a good memory and go there.'

The door opened and Zaydain merely stood holding it while Baduwa and Utibe obediently walked out through it.

'You too,' said Zaydain, pointing at Lo. Rosie looked in horror at Lo's terrified face as he stood cowering by his mattress. Zaydain shouted at him to hurry but Lo's feet seemed glued to the spot. Rosie walked over to Lo and knelt down in front of him.

'You have to go or he'll hurt you. I'll be waiting here when you get back,' she said, hugging him. She knew he probably didn't understand but hoped her voice would reassure him. She stood and held his hand, walking him to where Zaydain stood waiting, and as the door slammed, Rosie was left standing in a sea of clothes and sadness.

The time went painfully slowly as Rosie waited for them to return. She felt like a concerned mother whose children were out late at night, except that it wasn't late at night, it was the middle of the day which meant they had been taken to someone's house like she had been. Flashes of what had happened to her came and went at will, mostly when she was trying to think of something else. She conjured the image of her family again but the faces kept changing to those of the men in the house, their leering expressions bearing down on her. She tried to shake them out of her head by reciting song lyrics and quoting from her favourite movies, but nothing seemed to clear her mind. She longed for a distraction, anything.

Rosie fetched her own clothes from beside her mattress; at least they would be more comfortable than the ones she was still wearing. She shook out the jeans in an attempt to expel some of the grime and as she did so a piece of paper fluttered to the floor. She picked it up wondering what it could be and saw the photograph of Ted she had pocketed in his room all that time ago. She gasped as the memory chased the breath from her body and forced her to the floor. And suddenly she was fighting for air, tears pouring down her face. Every childhood memory flickered through her mind as she fought to capture each one and hold it close before they were lost amongst other things she would rather forget.

After a long time Rosie peeled herself off the floor and put on her clothes. She wandered over to the window. Her reflection was faint in the glass but she didn't look too closely, instead looking past into the now grey day. Beyond the high metal gate that bounded her prison was a narrow street, and beyond that cars and people rushed along the road, so oblivious to the nightmare that was unfolding just a short distance from them. Directly across the road she could see a small boutique shop, and a café, simply called The Tea Rooms. As she gazed at the glass front that listed 'Coffee, Tea, Cakes and other Sweet Delights', Rosie found herself longing for a chocolate milkshake, the kind with whipped cream and marshmallows.

Suddenly the door opened. It was Griff. He looked sheepishly into the room and then shut the door behind him. In his hand was a can of fizzy drink and a chocolate bar. He handed both to Rosie who took them gratefully.

'Thank you.'

Griff nodded but still would not meet her eye. Rosie stood feeling awkward, embarrassed by her tear-stained face and unsure of what he wanted as he looked around the room and back at her, not leaving.

'C-can I sit with you f-for a bit?' he stammered, twisting his hands together. Rosie was so surprised she just said of course and gestured to her mattress for him to sit on. Rosie guessed the other men must have taken Baduwa, Utibe and Lo out and left Griff to guard her.

Something suddenly occurred to Rosie and her heart started pounding as she desperately thought how she could do it.

'Would you like some?' she asked, opening her drink and sitting down.

He shook his head.

'What about some chocolate?' Griff nodded at that and Rosie broke him off a piece. He nibbled it like a mouse as Rosie took large bites, letting the delicious sweetness fill her swollen mouth.

Rosie took a deep breath; it was now or never. 'So, do you have a girlfriend?'

Griff shook his head, covering his ears as if he didn't want to hear her questions.

'Surely you must. Or maybe you really like a girl?' Rosie pushed.

Griff shook his head.

Rosie gasped theatrically. 'I knew it, there is a girl you like! What's her name?'

Griff pulled his jumper over his face, and Rosie feared she might have pushed too far too soon.

'Do you get the chance to take girls out?' she persevered. 'You seem to be very busy with work most of the time.'

Griff peeped out through the neck of his jumper and looked down at his feet.

'Zaydain doesn't let me out.'

'Is Zaydain your boss then?' probed Rosie.

Griff shook his head. 'Brother.'

Of course, thought Rosie, no wonder someone like Griff was involved. He didn't have any choice.

Rosie took a deep breath again. 'Maybe you could take me out sometime?'

Griff looked at her then and shook his head vigorously, fear in his eyes.

'Perhaps if I spoke to Zaydain he might let you take me out for a little while, when I'm better. Perhaps next time they're all out and it's just you and me?'

Griff continued to shake his head.

'Don't worry, you leave it with me,' said Rosie, trying to sound decisive. 'Don't tell anyone we had this little chat. I'll tell him it was my idea and that it would make you so happy.'

A smile snuck across Griff's face but it was quickly gone as he stood to leave.

'I have to go. Zaydain'll be back soon.'

Rosie nodded and stood up to give him a hug. He was stiff and awkward but when she pulled away he was smiling.

If nothing else, thought Rosie as he left the room, she'd given him something to hope for, not to mention the hope she'd given herself.

# Chapter 14

Ted's face itched beneath the facial prosthetic and whatever else Saffron had used to change his face so radically. He longed to scratch at it but had been forbidden under pain of death, so he could only contort his face for relief.

It had taken six hours to get him looking like William Hungerford, and now, as he walked to the nightclub he kept catching his reflection in windows and freaking himself out. The transformation really was amazing. Saffron had made a mould of his face and then used the mould to literally build a mask that he would be able to peel off and put back on each day. She'd layered up his cheeks to fill them out, built around his eyes to make them appear sunken. Then all he'd needed was a large pair of wire-rimmed glasses and a moustache. He had to wear a wig, of course, as William's hair was thinner and greyer than Ted's, but the suit fitted perfectly with just a little padding needed for his bum and stomach.

Ted's audience had been just as impressed with his make-up, not to mention with Blue clapping and twirling her excitement around the room. Ted had completely fallen in love with her fairy-like qualities and her total lack of inhibition. Most of the girls he knew were interested in the same boring things but Blue was unlike any girl he had ever seen and he found himself resenting Trig for not appearing to appreciate her as much as Ted knew he would if she were his.

William had cowered in the corner of the room with Bill holding his face towards the light for Saffron to copy. Ted had stared at his wobbling mouth with disgust, hating him for everything his sister was going through. As far as Ted was concerned he represented all the filthy perverts that inhabited the sewers of society.

They had all asked William questions about the life he led. He'd refused to say anything until Bill had gently persuaded him it was in his best interest, and then he'd blubbed like a baby, snot and spit splattering his pathetic face, the truth spilling out like vomit. How he'd been 'engaging' children from the club for over a year; how sometimes there were familiar faces, ones he requested again if he'd liked them, but mostly it was a high turnover and he never knew what he was going to get. The children would be paraded around in front of him and others like him, and then they would engage them for however long they wanted to pay for, either then and there or at another time. He swore initially he had no idea where the children came from but with a squeeze from Bill, he soon confessed that he knew that most of them were trafficked into the country from abroad. Ted pushed him for information of any British children and he'd said there were sometimes more 'local' kids, as he put it, but not that often, mostly because they cost more and the risk involved in using them was greater.

Ted felt ashamed as he remembered the moment he lost it on William, how he'd leapt up from the chair, face half done, and pounded on him. He suddenly had no control of his rage and wanted to punish William for all the pain his sister was in, all the desperation he felt, and for the hell his parents were going through. Trig let it play out for a while but then had Bill pull Ted off, saying he didn't want his face unrecognisable for Saffron to copy.

Ted was so shaken afterwards that they'd had to have a break as the scowl on his face made it impossible for Saffron to work on.

Now that Ted was standing at the entrance to The Lock he felt no better than William Hungerford, like he was wearing his perverseness as well as his face.

The bouncer nodded in recognition and let him straight in. Once inside Ted followed the directions they'd forced out of William; going down one flight of stairs and then along behind the balcony to where a large curtain hung.

As the music kept time to his beating heart, Ted waited while the bouncers shone a black light on the key around his neck to illuminate the number. They then looked him up on the computer; nodding him through when they were satisfied he was William Hungerford.

Ted was whisked to a central table as soon as he walked through the door, and asked if he'd like his usual. Ted suspected William's usual would be as vomit-inducing as him but he nodded. As he gazed at the sea of girls parading and dancing around the floor, each one seemed to have Rosie's face, her immature body, her innocent smile, and Ted felt anxiety surging through his chest. How could he do this? How could he pretend to be William?

Ted saw a man push one of the girls towards him and he held his breath as she walked over, her eyes on the floor, her hands clenched at her sides.

'Hello, Mister. You remember me?'

Ted opened his mouth to speak but nothing came out. The girl looked up expectantly and her soft brown eyes were so sad that Ted had to look away.

'Yes of course. What was your name again?'

'Mai-Li,' the girl replied.

Ted spied the familiar key around her neck.

'You like me today?' she asked.

'I haven't decided what I feel like today,' Ted whispered, hardly believing what was coming out of his mouth. 'I will call you over later if I'd like to see you again.'

The girl nodded and went to report back to the man who had sent her over. She looked so tiny standing next to him.

Ted's drink arrived and he sipped it hesitantly. It was as he suspected; sickly sweet and revolting, but he had to pretend it was what he had been waiting for all day – that, and these tempting morsels in front of him. He concentrated on his drink, unsure of what to do, feeling expectant eyes on him as if waiting for him to make a move. Everything seemed to pulse in slow motion; lights in his eyes, girls dancing, music pounding, the room spinning. Suddenly the need to be somewhere else took over and he stood up and went to the gents.

Shutting the cubicle door behind him he took several deep breaths. *Get a grip!* he hissed at himself, banging his fist against the door. He was going to blow his cover if he didn't pull himself together. There was no sign of Rosie, and Ted knew it would be suspicious if he just sat waiting all night. He thought back to Mai-Li: her timid, frightened eyes; her tiny, innocent body. Suddenly an idea gripped him; maybe he could help both of them.

Back at the table, Ted signalled to Mai-Li, asking her very politely if he could engage her that night, if it wasn't too much trouble. She led him up some stairs and along a corridor with many doors. The room they entered was very basic: one queen-size bed, one chair, one bedside table with a bowl of condoms on it. Ted felt himself blush under his mask and for the first time was glad he was wearing it.

Mai-Li sat on the bed, presumably waiting for William to say what he desired of her, but Ted merely sat next to her and held his breath. He hadn't worked out what he would do once they got to the room. He could feel Mai-Li glance up at him expectantly. Slowly he saw her hand reach towards his face. Ted jumped but she left her hand there, pinching his cheek gently. Then she looked afraid and moved further away.

'It's a mask,' Ted rushed.

Mai-Li seemed nervous so Ted quickly continued.

'My name is Ted, I'm trying to find my little sister. She was kidnapped a while ago and someone tipped me off that she may be at The Lock but she wasn't here tonight and I didn't know what to do so thought I should do what William normally does and engage a girl, which turned out to be you,' rushed Ted.

Ted searched Mai-Li's face for a sign that she wasn't going to run out of the room screaming and blow his cover. But instead she moved closer again and touched his cheek, pulling harder this time so that it moulded between her fingers.

'Careful, I need to leave here looking the same,' said Ted, gently removing her hand. 'Please don't tell; I need to come back again tomorrow and for the next few days and see if she appears. I was hoping I could engage you every day, then at least I wouldn't draw any unnecessary attention and you would have a few hours just in here with me. You could sleep or do whatever you want.'

Ted looked anxiously at Mai-Li waiting for her to respond, but she quickly nodded and Ted relaxed a little.

'There was a white girl at The Lock not long ago,' said Mai-Li in a quiet voice.

'Really?' said Ted excitedly. 'Did she have shoulder length blonde hair and blue eyes?'

'No, she had short brown hair with a fringe, like this,' Mai-Li indicated a line across her forehead. 'She was with two black girls. She looked new though, like she didn't know what she was doing, yer know? It's easy to spot the new girls.'

'Girl with short brown hair,' Ted repeated under his breath. 'Either there are more white girls involved than the police had suggested, or it was Rosie in a wig,' he said, more to himself than Mai-Li. 'Of course! I saw her come out of the club. Two black girls you say?' said Ted enthusiastically. 'You think it could be her? Do they ever make you wear a wig?'

'No, but they're not trying to hide me from anyone. No one is looking for me,' Mai-Li replied.

Ted looked at her apologetically; he was forgetting her in his excitement.

Could it really have been Rosie? Was he that close to finding her? Did he dare to hope that this nightmare might come to an end? Ted wanted to jump up and hug Mai-Li, tear off his stupid mask and do the chicken dance. But then another thought occurred to him: if that had been Rosie then she had been just a few feet away from him and he hadn't even seen her. He had looked right through her as if she were a ghost. He had to be more vigilant. The traffickers were not leaving anything to chance, they had created an illusion to entice the punters and deter the authorities. And they were good at it.

***

For the next few days Ted returned to The Lock as William Hungerford. Despite the new-found hope he had, Ted wasn't going to let his naivety make him miss Rosie again. He scanned every face and body of every person that entered his sights. He questioned everyone he could without alerting suspicion. He became the man that his disguise allowed, and was surprised at the accessibility that permitted him.

But somehow it wasn't enough. The final day came and went without a single sighting of Rosie and Ted felt himself returning to the young, inexperienced kid that he really was.

As he stood outside The Lock for the last time, hands on his knees, waiting for the sick feeling to pass, he felt the threatening tears burn his eyes. He rubbed them away angrily; what right did he have to cry? He was safe, unharmed, free. It was Rosie who should be crying, probably was; would be if she only knew what a useless idiot he really was. And on top of that he'd had to leave Mai-Li there, trapped in the same terrifying world as Rosie because he couldn't help her, not yet. He'd promised Mai-Li that as soon as he found Rosie he would be back to get her, he just didn't want to expose the one place that Rosie had been seen and ruin his chances of picking up her trail again at some point.

'Hard night?' came a voice nearby.

Ted looked up from under his aching brow.

Standing in front of him, one eyebrow raised, was a girl who couldn't have been much older than him. Ted's eyes drank in her student-like appearance; her long hair tied messily back, her jeans and denim jacket combo. Her expression was that of amusement as she studied him back.

Ted stuttered over his words, completely taken off guard.

'I… umm, I… I don't know what you mean. I just felt a bit nauseous if you must know.'

'It is all rather nauseating in there isn't it?' she agreed.

Ted looked at her in surprise. How did she know where he'd been?

'In where?' asked Ted, starting to walk away.

'Oh come on, you don't belong in a place like that.'

'I go there all the time, actually' Ted floundered. 'I enjoy it.'

The woman laughed loudly. Ted was beginning to wonder if she was some spy working for the club that kept an eye out for phoneys like him. She just kept smiling at him and Ted felt totally exposed, like she was seeing right through him.

'Who are you?' he asked, irritated.

'My name is Martha Mayhew. I'm a journalist.'

Ted took a step backwards. He felt like he'd been busted for something he hadn't even done. The confusion on his face made Martha smile even more and her amusement was really starting to get on Ted's nerves. Ted turned and began to walk away.

'Don't go, Ted, let's get a coffee and have a chat,' said Martha from behind him, her Doc Martens thumping impatiently on the pavement as she tried to keep up.

'I don't have anything to say to you,' he replied, turning down a busier street to try and lose her in the crowds. Then he froze.

'What did you just call me?' he asked, turning to face her as she skidded to a halt just inches from him.

She regained her composure quickly. 'I called you Ted,' she replied.

'But my name is William Hungerford,' said Ted forcefully.

'Maybe for tonight but normally your name is Ted. Look there's no need for this, I'm happy to come clean with what I know and why I'm here but I'd prefer to do it somewhere more private.'

Ted looked into her seemingly innocent green eyes and nodded, following her into a dimly lit bar with old-style blues music trickling from one of the crackling speakers. They ordered drinks and found a seat in a corner away from prying eyes and ears – although who would care what they were up to Ted wasn't sure, but it all felt suitable to the situation.

Ted waited patiently for Martha to talk. She seemed to be taking her time removing her jacket and rummaging in her bag and then sipping her drink, but eventually she looked up at Ted and smiled.

'I have a brother in the police force. He happened to mention your sister's case to me because I have been working on a piece about child trafficking. It's taking longer than anticipated because it's such a hard thing to keep track of; it's all so underground and un-policed that no one really knows the full extent of the problem. Your sister's case is the first one I have heard about that has a beginning to it, a source. Most of the kids have been in the "system" for ages and their history is untraceable because of the hidden nature of child trafficking and exploitation.'

Martha stopped to take a sip of her drink. Ted waited for her to continue but she seemed to have finished.

'What exactly is it you're reporting on?' asked Ted impatiently.

'Well, up until I heard about your sister it was all just snippets from various websites and a few interviews with charity workers. I knew child trafficking was big business but there are so few sources of information. Victims are generally too traumatised to talk about their experiences and no one seems able to catch the traffickers themselves, so I've been rummaging in the dark, so to speak. I'm kinda new to the journalism thing and I wanted to make a good first impression… well, actually, I'm really just studying journalism,' she said sheepishly.

Ted frowned. So she was a student. Great, their story would end up in some student rag, most likely used to mop up sick after a heavy night out.

'But I'd really like to tell Rosie's and your story,' she rushed. 'I'd do a good job. And there are some of our stories that make it to the tabloids, if our tutors think they're good enough, so it's a start.'

Ted studied her anxious face for a moment as her pleading eyes bore into his. It was hard to resist her and he eventually found himself nodding goofily like one of those dogs in car windows. Anyway, he thought, any extra help could only be a good thing. She whooped and threw her arms around him across the table. Ted froze in surprise and she quickly let go, looking embarrassed.

Martha pulled out a pad and pen and held them poised.

'What?' asked Ted. 'You mean now?'

'Oh, sorry, did you have somewhere else to be?' she asked coyly.

'I wouldn't mind taking this old face off,' he replied.

'Yes, well, we all have things we'd rather be doing, I'm sure Rosie does too.'

# Chapter 15

It was the end of a long week for Rosie. She had been locked in the room for six days and the walls were starting to bear down on her, close in and crush her. But, as she kept telling herself, anything was better than being engaged every day like the others had. Each day they came back a little less complete, like bits of them were being slowly chipped away. Baduwa had lost her glow of hope and colour, although she tried to be brave – for Utibe, Rosie guessed – but it was like seeing a bird who had lost its feathers and yet was still trying to preen them. Utibe no longer made eye contact with any of them; shutting herself away in her own little world where no one could get to her – a place Rosie knew well. And Lo woke in the night screaming, fighting to get out of the nightmare he was trapped in. Rosie felt helpless as she watched each of them deal with their own horror the only way they could. She wondered if they now even envied her injuries if it meant they could stay behind as she had, but Rosie knew her time was nearly up; the bruises had almost gone and she suspected Zaydain would want to make back any losses, and fast.

Griff had spent a little time with her each day when the others were out and Rosie tried to probe him gently for information, but he wouldn't speak about what they did; merely shaking his head as he pressed his lips together. But Rosie could tell there was something very wrong with Griff, he didn't function like a normal adult; he was almost more of a child than Rosie. Did he even know what was happening here? Did he understand everything his brother made him do?

Rosie now sat waiting, as she had every day after the others had been taken to their engagements, for Griff's usual visit. This could be her last chance to persuade him, she had to give it a go at least. Griff entered the room as usual with a bar of chocolate and a drink. Rosie took them gratefully and offered some to him. As they sat munching in silence Rosie suddenly began to get cold feet. What if he didn't agree? What if he told Zaydain that she had tried to escape? Would that put her family in danger? But she had no choice. There was no way anyone was going to find her without another clue, and no other way she could think of to let anyone who might be looking for her know where she was. It was a long shot anyway but she had to try something, so she took a deep breath.

'I spoke to Zaydain last night, about you taking me out, and he said you could. He said they would be out for most of the day today and that we could go for a coffee together whilst they were gone. He doesn't want the others to know though, in case they start asking to go out too,' Rosie finished, swallowing her heart back down.

Griff looked at her, a slight smile playing on his lips. It seemed like he might burst out laughing and tell her that she must think he was stupid to let her out. But as Rosie watched his face she could see each thought change his facial expression and suddenly he was looking sad.

'Not allowed coffee.'

'Well I don't think he meant us to have coffee necessarily, it's just a figure of speech,' Rosie rushed. 'They sell other drinks. What do you like to drink?'

Griff started shaking his head again and Rosie feared she'd already blown it.

'What about tea?' Rosie asked.

Griff shook his head more.

Rosie felt desperation tighten her skin.

'They don't only sell hot drinks you know, perhaps you'd like an apple juice or a Coke?'

Griff shook his head more and Rosie cursed at herself as she remembered he never had any of the drinks he bought her. She wracked her brain, desperately thinking of something else to lure him. Then she had an idea.

'What about chocolate milkshake?'

Rosie held her breath, watching him. He stopped shaking his head and looked at her, a smile creeping across his face, lighting it in a way Rosie had not seen before. He nodded excitedly and stood up. Rosie's heart leapt. She jumped to her feet and headed straight for the door. Could this at last be her chance? She dared to let herself hope it could be it, as she imagined the looks on her family's faces when they saw her. She'd blow the lid on this sordid world wide open for everyone to see. She pictured her face in the newspapers, on TV, her family crying as they spoke of the hell they had been through. It all felt within her grasp as Rosie almost skipped down the steps leading out of the block of flats. She could hear Griff panting with excitement on her heels. If she could just leave the picture somewhere where Ted might spot it, then he'd know. Her mind started running wild: maybe she should make a run for it. Why leave a clue when she could just bolt? She wanted to run right now and never stop, scream at the top of her voice until someone came to her rescue.

But as she stepped outside she didn't recognise this new world, the one she used to be a part of. The buildings looked more sinister, each face that passed her seemed threatening. How could she trust anyone now? For all she knew they were all in on it. She glanced at Griff as he pulled up alongside her. He looked skinny and feeble, vulnerable even, but this was his world and she couldn't be sure he wasn't as much of an illusion as the rest of it. Every bone in Rosie's body was screaming at her to run, but her head was so full of doubt and confusion. For now all she could do was keep the café in her sights and walk as if through a tunnel towards it. That was her goal right now, anything else felt impossible.

They entered the café that Rosie had looked longingly at so many times and found a table in the corner by the window. The café was small, only big enough for about ten tables, and each one felt too close, like it was trying to block her in, stop her from escaping. Rosie concentrated on breathing, and looked around her for a suitable place to hide the picture. She spotted a plant behind her on the windowsill and decided that would be perfect, as the picture would only be seen from the outside and so was less likely to be removed by anyone in the café.

A waitress appeared at the table, barely meeting their eyes as they ordered their milkshakes. She looked bored, distracted, probably wishing she was somewhere else. But Rosie realised she would give anything to be that waitress right now; to slip into her scruffy Converse, and wait on everyone and anyone all day, hour after hour, if only it meant she didn't have to go back.

Griff's expectant gaze followed the waitress as she went to prepare their order, and Rosie took the chance to reach into her pocket and take out the photograph. She unfolded it under the table and checked the number was still there: fifty-five was scratched discreetly in the bottom left hand corner. Rosie glanced at Griff to be sure he was still distracted and reached behind her and placed the photo next to the pot plant and against the window. But as she pulled her hand away it felt like such a feeble attempt. What were the chances, really, of Ted spotting a small photo in one of the hundreds of cafes in London? What could possibly bring him here of all places? But she had to try, there might never be another opportunity.

Rosie was suddenly aware that Griff was wriggling in his chair and figured their drinks must be coming. Trying to catch the waitress's eye as she approached the table, Rosie longed for her to notice this odd pairing, to get suspicious and call the police. But there was nothing remotely observant there as she placed the drinks in front of them.

Rosie looked around the room. Aside from them, there was an old man falling asleep in his teacup at one table, and a woman feeding her baby at another. She could see the toilet just beyond the counter, behind which the waitress now stood staring absently into space. Maybe she could go to the loo and whisper to the waitress to call the police as she passed. Would Griff notice? She couldn't be sure, although looking at his milk-covered top lip stretched wide in a huge grin of pleasure he seemed more of a child than a threat. Rosie tried to guess how old he was. He had lines around his eyes and his hair was thin on the top so she guessed he must at least be in his thirties, but his eyes held intelligence that wasn't reflected in his appearance, much like some animals.

A loud slurping signalled that time was running out.

'Griff, I'm just going to the Ladies, OK?' Rosie said, standing.

Griff nodded and carried on sucking every last drop from his glass.

Rosie walked quickly towards the toilet, her heart pounding as she neared the waitress. Just as she pulled level and was about to whisper to her to call the police, a shout came from the kitchen and she scuttled out. Rosie bolted into the toilet and shut the door. She'd missed her chance.

She sat down to catch her breath and calm her nerves. Her shuddering body was making the seat rattle and she could now hear the voice that had shouted at the waitress telling her to stop standing around and do some work.

There was only one option left; she had to run for it. It was so risky but the thought of going back there, facing more men like the ones that had hurt her, was more than she could bear. And she would kick herself for missing the opportunity if she didn't at least try. If she could just get a head start then maybe, just maybe, she could outrun Griff.

Rosie stood on her shuddering legs and peeped out through the door. Her path was clear to the exit. She looked over at Griff and saw he was on the phone. Could he have got suspicious and be calling Zaydain or Gabriel? She wasn't going to wait and find out; it was now or never. She took a deep breath, checked Griff was looking away and walked briskly towards the exit.

Suddenly the waitress was standing in front of her blocking the way.

'Not leaving without paying, I hope,' she said, one eyebrow raised suspiciously.

'No, of course not,' Rosie almost whispered. 'My friend is paying.' She nodded in Griff's direction as she tried to get past the waitress.

'He doesn't seem to be the type to pay,' said the waitress, looking over at Griff who was no longer on the phone and appeared to be using the straw from his drink to contact other life forms.

Rosie saw an opportunity.

'Please, help me. That man has kidnapped me and I need to get away, now. Can you call the police? I'm being held against my will,' she whispered urgently.

The waitress sighed. 'Really? You expect me to believe that whilst you're heading out the door without paying? You want me to go back there and use the phone while you run off? Please, do I look like a dumb-ass to you, sister?'

Rosie looked at the waitress in despair. Why was she not helping?

Rosie couldn't wait around trying to convince her, she had to go. Pushing past the waitress, she reached for the door handle.

'Oy, Bob!' shouted the waitress. 'This girl's trying to leave without paying!'

The moment hung suspended in the air as Rosie froze in panic, like someone had paused the terrifying scene to savour her agony. Then they hit play again and the place erupted as she pulled at the door with all her strength against the resisting hand of the waitress and raced out through it.

Shouting broke out behind her as chairs fell in what she suspected was Griff's haste to chase after her. She wanted to stop and go back and say she'd made a horrible mistake and wasn't really intending to run away, but her feet seemed to have other ideas as they followed one another faster than she thought they could carry her, along the pavement, past some shops and a pub.

The skin on her back rippled and fizzed as if Griff's breath was already bearing down on her; the fear that he could be so close spurring her momentum. She couldn't imagine how her legs were holding her up, it felt like they were someone else's as her pounding feet carried her across a road, past a cemetery on her right and a church on her left, and then into a park. Rosie wasn't convinced it was a good idea to go into the park as there were less people there, but it was an open space where she hoped she could gather speed.

She could hear her breath rasping through her chest and her heart panting to keep up. Or was that someone else panting? Heavy footsteps pounded the tarmac behind her. Was that Griff? Could it be the owner of the café? Rosie didn't dare look back to see as she ran over an iron bridge that straddled a stagnant canal, and then past an aviary. She could see brightly coloured birds fluttering in the run-down cages, looking so out of place with their beautiful bright plumage against the dreary grey backdrop of a London sky. Her dash past seemed to send them into a flurry of feathers and squawks, their cries echoing her wheezing breath.

In front of her was a fountain surrounded by pigeons that flew into the air as she ran through, scattering like rice at a wedding. Rosie instinctively put her arms up to protect her face, momentarily blinded and slowed by their awkwardness. She wanted to stop, catch her breath, and work out where she was going, but there was no going back as the birds returned to earth, closing the curtain behind her.

Up ahead, Rosie caught sight of a bus and realised there was a road right in front of her. If she could just make it to that gate and out into the road, someone would have to notice her. The thought that this might be it, the end to it all, whatever that may be, gave her the final push she needed.

Racing through the gate, she closed her eyes and launched herself into the road. There was a screeching of brakes and then all went quiet.

***

Rosie wasn't sure how much time had gone by but she was definitely lying on something very hard and there were voices all around her.

'Mum, Dad,' she whispered.

'I'm here, darling,' came a man's voice.

'Daddy?'

'Yes, sweetheart.'

It didn't sound much like her dad's voice but all the sounds seemed distorted. Rosie smiled as the relief washed over her. Her dad had found her.

# Chapter 16

It was morning by the time Ted and Martha had finished exchanging stories, and the copious cups of coffee coupled with the lack of sleep had started to make vision and speech challenging, so they'd decided to part company and meet up again after some rest.

Ted now stood on the Tube, squashed between the door and a commuter's rucksack, his eyes barely focussing. His face felt horrible underneath the make-up and he was dying to take it off. He hadn't dared to try in the café in case it didn't all come away, and then he'd have had half a face hanging off him like something from a horror film.

It had been horrendous to listen to what Martha had told him about trafficking, how it was the second largest form of illegal trade in the world, after drugs, and that the authorities really had no clue how to stop it happening. She'd said that about half of the people trafficked were children, mostly from poor, third-world countries, but sometimes not; it was nearly as common for children to be trafficked internally in a country like Britain, especially if no one cared that the child had been taken, or had profited from it. And sometimes, even children travelling abroad with their families were targeted.

Ted was horrified that something so evil and so prevalent wasn't headline news all the time. He kept asking Martha why there weren't more shocking stories in the newspapers and on the news, ones that would frighten people into doing something about it. But Martha had just shrugged and said that was what she was hoping to achieve with her research, or at least to raise awareness.

Ted looked around him on the Tube, at the faces that wouldn't look back at him. He tried to imagine what each person was going to do that day by the clothes they were wearing: the suits usually meant a business, office job of some kind. The more casual and trendy could be for the more creative jobs. Then there were the downright scruffy who could only be the labourers. Or maybe not. Perhaps the suits were the unemployed going for interviews. The casual trendy ones were merely shopping using their fathers' credit cards, and the scruffy could all be going into the office for dress-down Friday. Ted decided there was no way to tell, and any of them could be hiding Rosie or exploiting other children, and that was what he was really trying to work out.

The Tube screeched to a halt and Ted tumbled out, unaware his legs had gone to sleep. Commuters grumbled and groaned at his clumsiness, and Ted wondered if they'd have been so rude if he wasn't a fat, ugly, balding dude in a badly fitting suit. He suspected they would have been more afraid of upsetting the angry teenager that he was underneath, if only they knew.

As Ted walked in through the door of Dillon's house the familiar smell of a fried breakfast hit him and he realised how hungry he was. Fortunately Mrs M was privy to the William Hungerford operation, otherwise seeing a dishevelled bald man walk through her door uninvited at seven in the morning might have given her a small heart attack. But as it was she simply laughed, as she always did when she saw Ted coming home looking so completely out of character.

'Just in time for breakfast, my love.' She grinned. 'Perhaps you'd like to change first?'

Ted nodded and staggered up the stairs. He could hear the shower running as he peeled off his face and chucked it on the table in Dillon's room. It was so surreal to be removing his face but he'd started to get used to it and now found it hard to remember who he was at any one time. And although they had had no luck finding Rosie, he was pleased to be rid at last of what he feared was becoming his alter ego.

Dillon walked into the room with just a towel on and smiled at Ted.

'You missed a bit,' he said, pointing to his eyebrows.

Ted tried to smile and peeled them off, tossing them on the side with his fat face.

'So how'd it go last night?' Dillon asked. 'You've never been out all night before, is that a good sign?'

Ted shook his head. 'Unfortunately not.' He sighed. 'Still no sign of Rosie, but I did meet a girl–'

'Oh yeah?' Dillon interrupted, his eyebrows raised suggestively.

'Not like that, you muppet. She was a reporter actually. Turns out she's been following Rosie's case, off the record. She's actually a student and her brother's a copper and he tips her off about cases, and she was doing an assignment about child trafficking and he told her about Rosie.'

'So she could be helpful?'

'Dunno. Apart from knowing more about the child trafficking world than I do, she hasn't any more leads. Although she had heard about The Lock, but only because she'd been following me, so she's about up to the same place as we are.'

'But now that she knows about The Lock she can tell her brother and they can bust the place can't they?'

'Apparently not. Remember Trig said it's owned by some "influential" people? Well, it's kind of untouchable at the moment, but Martha said she reckoned once her story was finished and out there, and the public got involved, that the police would have to react.'

'God it's a pile of shite this country, isn't it? What are we meant to do in the meantime?'

'I don't know, mate.' Ted shrugged. The feeling of hopelessness was threatening to overtake him again so Ted forced a smile, dressed quickly, and headed down for breakfast.

Just as he'd shovelled the first forkful into his ravenous mouth, his phone rang.

'Rosie's been found!' said Martha's excited voice on the end of the phone.

'What?' said Ted, practically spitting his food across the table.

'She's with your dad.'

'What? But he didn't call me.'

'Well I'm sure he's going to. He had to take her to the hospital first so he probably got caught up doing that.'

'The hospital? Is she OK?'

'As far as I know, yes. She was hit by a car, but apparently she wasn't badly hurt. And your dad was there and he took her to the hospital.'

'Dad was there? But…'

'I don't know the full story, Ted. My brother literally just called me and said that one of the witnesses had called the police when they recognised Rosie and said she'd been in an accident but that her dad was with her. That's all I know. I thought you'd be pleased and want to go and see her straight away.'

Ted shook his head. 'Yes of course, I've just got so used to asking questions all the time, I guess.' He laughed. 'I'll call Dad straight away and find out where they are. Thanks, Martha.'

'No problem, speak to you later.'

Ted hung up the phone and beamed at Dillon's smiling face.

'She's been found! Dad has her, apparently. Not sure how but I'll give him a call,' he said, suddenly laughing out loud and punching the air at the realisation that his little sister was safe at last.

Ted grinned at Dillon's mum as he dialled and saw tears glistening in her eyes.

'Dad? It's Ted! How's Rosie?' he rushed.

'What?' came his dad's surprised voice down the phone.

'Rosie! They said you found her.'

'What? Who said that?'

'My friend Martha, whose brother is a copper…'

'Who's Martha?'

'A journalist I met…'

'A journalist? You talking to the press now?'

'No, no,' said Ted hurriedly. 'I'll explain when I see you. Listen, she said that Rosie had been hit by a car and you'd been there,' said Ted, his voice rising with anticipation. He couldn't understand why his dad was asking so many silly and irrelevant questions.

'I haven't left the house since yesterday morning, Ted.'

Ted's hand dropped from his ear and hung limp at his side as what his dad said sank in. He couldn't believe he'd let himself hope without seeing her with his own eyes. He looked up and caught Dillon's look and then broke down. He felt Dillon take the phone from his hand and speak to his dad but it was just a murmur in the background. Ted's head was swimming and he felt like he was going to throw up. He sat on the chair, tears stinging his eyes as he began to sob uncontrollably. How could Martha have been so cruel as to tell him that Rosie had been found when she hadn't? Maybe she wasn't his friend after all. He was furious with her as he roughly wiped the tears from his eyes and grabbed his phone from Dillon, dialling Martha's number.

'Hello?'

Ted was surprised to feel pain at the sound of her voice but he tore into her anyway, asking her how she could get his hopes up like that when she hadn't checked her facts. How it was worse than not saying anything at all. All Martha could do was stammer surprise at the other end, but there was no forgiveness in Ted's voice and he didn't care. He never wanted to speak to her again and he told her so as he hung up and tossed the phone across the room.

Mrs M wrapped her huge mass around Ted as he sobbed.

# Chapter 17

Rosie's body felt like it might snap as Gabriel half pulled, half carried her across the park and away from the accident. Her head was pounding as she tried to remember what had happened and how it was Gabriel and not Griff that had chased her. How he'd peeled her off the road whilst his hand was clamped down on her arm aggressively, whispering threats in her ear so that she knew if she uttered one word about him not being her dad he would kill her. And apart from a few suggestions from people at the scene that she should perhaps go to the hospital, no one even challenged him.

Anyway, it was her fault. If she had timed her run into the traffic better she might have actually been hit by a car, as was her intention, and then her injuries would have warranted an ambulance. As it was, she merely bumped her head on the road as she tripped and was now being dragged, as if in rewind, along the path she had run only a few moments ago as a free woman.

They arrived back at the flat where Zaydain was pacing angrily along the balcony outside the door. He lunged at Rosie but Gabriel put his arm in the way.

'Not now!' he hissed.

'I knew it was a mistake to keep her. She's been more trouble than she's worth. I vote we get rid of her right now,' snarled Zaydain.

Rosie shrank back behind Gabriel's bulk, away from Zaydain's red-eyed stare.

'She's only been a problem because you're incapable of keeping her in check! How could you leave that halfwit in charge?' shouted Gabriel.

'I had no idea he would be stupid enough to let her out. Anyway, if you'd been here I wouldn't have had to leave her with him. What took you so long?'

'I was delayed, that's all. Get 'er inside,' Gabriel said, shoving Rosie towards Zaydain.

Rosie was pushed roughly through the door of the room. Baduwa, Utibe and Lo rushed to her side, questions pouring from Baduwa's mouth. Rosie could still hear Zaydain and Gabriel arguing outside the door and hushed Baduwa into silence as she strained to hear.

'She can't stay here, someone might have recognised you, or her. It's getting too risky. I told you it was a bad idea to deal in white meat!' shouted Zaydain.

'Calm down, we will get rid of her but not without making some money first. Leave it with me; I'll speak to a few people. In the meantime, keep your head down for a couple of days in case anyone's sniffing around.'

Rosie heard Zaydain grunt and then all went quiet. She turned her attention back to the others who were all waiting patiently to hear what had happened. As Rosie was telling them she broke out in a creeping, cold sweat at what would now be the consequences of her actions. She hadn't given enough thought to what might happen if she got caught, but of course they'd want to move her, and as quickly as possible. So even if Ted somehow ended up in the area, and then by some miracle spotted the picture in the window, she would no longer be at number fifty-five, and all it would have succeeded in doing was getting his hopes up, and for what?

She also dreaded to think of the trouble Griff was in, or what it would all now mean for Baduwa, Utibe and Lo. And her family! What would happen to them? She lay down, Lo resting his head on her thigh. What had she done?

Rosie must have fallen asleep because the sound of the door bursting open jolted her awake. Gabriel's vast size filled the entire doorway and Lo scrambled behind her.

Rosie sat up defiantly and stared him in the eye, hatred pouring from every inch of her.

'Get up, you're coming with me,' he growled, pointing at Rosie.

She held her ground and didn't move. There was no way she was going anywhere.

'Now!' he boomed, his voice making them all jump.

Rosie shook her head.

'I'm not leaving,' she whispered.

'Why? Because you'll miss all this?' Gabriel indicated around the room.

It wasn't as ridiculous as it sounded. If she couldn't go home she didn't want to go somewhere else where there would be more of the same but likely worse. And Baduwa, Utibe and Lo were all she had right now, and who would look after them if she left? Who would make sure they were OK?

Plus she knew Griff, Zaydain and Rusty enough to know that although they had put her through what they had, she was sure they weren't the worst of what was out there.

'I want to stay here. I promise to be good,' assured Rosie, searching Gabriel's eyes for an ounce of compassion.

'Well that's touching but you're practically bought and paid for so up yer get,' he said, reaching forward and pulling Rosie to her feet. She struggled against his grip but it was no use. Rosie looked back at Baduwa, Utibe and Lo as she was dragged out of the room; each sobbing, they ran towards her.

'Let me say goodbye, at least,' screamed Rosie.

But Gabriel slammed the door, and they were gone.

Rosie cried uncontrollably, biting, scratching, kicking. If only she'd kept her head down and done as she was told none of this would be happening; she shouldn't have run, she should have trusted that Ted and her parents would find her, and just been patient. When would she ever learn?

Rosie caught Gabriel's eye in the mirror as the car swung out of the gate, and the hatred she saw there took her breath away. No one had ever looked at her with that much revulsion, not even her parents after she'd been arrested, or any of the other times she'd let them down. She hated thinking about how she'd behaved back then. Her mum and dad loved her and wanted the best for her and all she did was resent them.

Rosie tried to keep track of where they were driving. She recognised certain areas they passed; some she'd been to with Ted, most of them with her so-called mates. She knew enough to know they were crossing London from the north to the south, at least, and hoped they would end up somewhere she had been before so maybe she wouldn't feel so lost.

As they crossed the river, lights were starting to appear on the surface of the water, and Rosie realised yet another day was ending and she was still no better off than the day before. It didn't matter what was happening to her, time marched on regardless, taking with it innocence and youth, even people's memory of her. Her parents would likely be relieved she hadn't been found; after all, she'd been nothing but trouble to them anyway. And Ted would be able to get on with his life without always feeling responsible for her. Maybe it was time to accept this was her life now.

As the car finally pulled up outside a large house, Rosie figured they were somewhere south of Brixton, possibly Streatham, but it wasn't familiar territory to her. The eerie house stood on the edge of a busy road and looked completely out of place nestled amongst some trees with only dirt for a garden. To Rosie it looked like a run-down, haunted house that had been dropped in the wrong location, like the house that fell on the witch in the *Wizard of Oz*. Opposite, on the other side of the road, was a large housing estate that blocked out any remaining light the trees had allowed to pass.

Gabriel opened her door and she looked up at the house that loomed over her. Good things could not possibly happen here, she thought, but then what was she expecting?

Three stone steps led up to the door and Rosie tripped up all of them landing in a heap at the top. She couldn't work out why her legs refused to function. Gabriel didn't pay her any attention as he rang the doorbell, and Rosie scrambled to her feet just as the door opened. A small man, not much taller than Rosie, stood in front of them, his hair barely covered the top of his head and he had a moustache that lay menacingly above his top lip. Moustaches had always given Rosie the creeps.

Gabriel pushed Rosie through the door and the creepy man slammed it, presumably aware of her predisposition to flight.

'Your room is upstairs, I'll show you,' he said finally, his nasally, high-pitched voice echoing through the empty hall, piggy eyes glinting at her in the semi-darkness.

He led her slowly up the wooden stairs and onto the first floor. Unlocking the door he pushed it open and stood aside for Rosie to go in first. There was a bedroom in front of them, which, to Rosie's surprise, actually contained beds rather than just mattresses. Two of them were occupied by bodies and two were empty. The bodies stirred and looked up at Rosie; both girls and both white – not British, she didn't think, but definitely European. They quickly turned away disinterested, and the creepy man pointed Rosie towards one of the beds.

'You make your own food in the kitchen,' said the man, indicating the other room. 'And you clean up after yourself. Showers are only between the hours of six and seven, am and pm. Laundry you must do in the basin. You stay in here until I come and get you. Make no noise or there will be trouble.'

The man finished almost triumphantly, as if job well done, and strode out of the room, locking the door behind him.

Rosie perched on the bed unsure what to do. Neither of the girls turned around to face her again, so she decided to explore. In the next-door room she found a small cooker, a fridge, a kettle and a few pans and plates, all of which looked like they had, at best, been licked clean by an animal. There was also a table and four chairs. The lino flooring was torn and sparse, and the floorboards that showed beneath looked damp and rotten. Rosie made a mental note not to stand on anything but the few remaining bits of plastic flooring in case she ended up back in the hall downstairs.

She noted porridge, rice, and tins of lentils, pasta, tinned tomatoes, and bread, then long-life milk and cheese in the fridge. This was positively gourmet compared to what she'd been used to, but she hoped one of the other girls knew how to cook because she had no idea what to do with the ingredients they were expected to work with. Assuming, as it was getting late, that the girls would have eaten already, Rosie pulled herself off a chunk of bread and a piece of cheese and contented herself with that for her dinner.

As she was eating she heard movement coming from the bedroom. There was no talking, just knocking and banging and shuffling. She heard the toilet flush. Then a key turned in the lock and the creepy man entered. He didn't say anything, just stood in the doorway as if waiting for something. Both girls walked out of the bedroom, their high heels clacking on the floor, their legs bare but for very short skirts. They turned in Rosie's direction, their faces expressionless, and left the flat, leaving Rosie alone once more.

# Chapter 18

When Ted awoke he felt terrible. His eyes were heavy and puffy and his head was pounding as if he'd had a really heavy night. He rolled off the sofa and looked at his phone to see the time. It said he had eleven missed calls, all from Martha. Ted felt a pang of guilt; he knew he'd been harsh with her and that she'd probably thought she was delivering the best news he'd ever heard.

It was late and there didn't appear to be anyone else in the house as Ted's tired and dishevelled body wandered into the kitchen. In true Mrs M style there was a plate of food on the table with an arrow next to it that pointed towards the microwave. Ted smiled as he heated the food, grateful that everyone else in his life was so amazing; his family, his friends, he was so lucky. He realised that with friends and family like he had it would have been easy to slip through life without witnessing anything as nasty as what was happening to his sister, if it hadn't happened to her. How easy it would be to be blinkered to all such horror as long as it always happened to someone else, and he never watched the news.

He looked out of the window as he waited for his food to heat up. There was no way to tell there was anything bad happening in the world at all: all he could see was someone parking their car; two people walking in through their front door; and a passing van with the driver on his phone. Ted knew there was a possibility that the van driver might be distracted by whoever he was talking to, mount the kerb and hit a pedestrian; that there may be burglars waiting inside that house and they may be armed; and that the guy parking his car may have just murdered someone and have the body stashed in the trunk. But as long as it wasn't happening to him or anyone he cared about, it was as easy to ignore as turning away from the window, taking his food out of the microwave and eating it. Which he did.

Just as he was finishing, his phone rang again. Ted looked at the screen; it was Martha. He took a deep breath,

'Hello?'

'Hi, Ted, it's Martha, don't hang up, I'm sorry, just give me a chance to explain,' she rushed.

Ted wanted to be angry with her but the sound of her voice so desperate melted his anger and he couldn't help smiling.

'I'm not going to hang up,' he said quietly.

'Oh God, Ted, I'm really sorry. I'm such an idiot. I should have checked that it was your dad before telling you. I just got so excited and wanted to tell you as soon as I heard. Turns out it was someone pretending to be your dad, but I guess you already know that. But at least the police have a description of who has her, so that's promising.'

'What does he look like?' Ted asked, cringing as he waited for her to reply.

Martha seemed to pause on the other end and Ted prepared for the worst. Although, thinking about it, was there any description she could give him that would reassure him and make it all OK? He thought not, unless she was being held by an enormous teddy bear.

'Tall guy; well over six foot. Shaved head, big build,' Martha said quietly. 'Someone that would stand out in a crowd at least, not your average forty-something white male. Certainly not average…' she trailed off.

'What was she doing there, does anyone know? Did she actually get hurt?' asked Ted, sitting down, exhausted again.

'Apparently she just ran into the road. Luckily she wasn't hit by a car, but she did fall and hurt her head. She was out cold for a few seconds.'

'But where did the man come from?'

'No one really knows; he was just there suddenly.' She paused. 'I have a theory though.'

'Go on.'

'Well, that he was chasing her. That she'd somehow managed to escape and he was chasing her across the park that was right there. And she threw herself into the road in a desperate attempt to get away from him and to attract attention. Unfortunately, these people are professionals and are usually prepared for all eventualities.'

Ted felt sick. His little sister, all alone, running for her life, and he wasn't there to protect her.

'Is there anything we can do?' Ted barely whispered.

'Not much… unless you want to go to the site of the accident and have a look around? She can't have run that far, maybe we could ask around, see if anyone saw anything.'

'We? You want to come?'

'Of course.' She paused. 'If that's OK?'

'Definitely,' said Ted, cheering up slightly. 'Where's the nearest Tube?'

'I'm not sure there is one, it's somewhere around Stoke Newington, but why don't I drive? Means we're more mobile. I'll pick you up in half an hour,' said Martha.

'OK, I'll give you the address…' but she'd hung up. Ted smiled as he realised she probably already knew where he was staying.

Ted only had time for a quick wash and change before an impatient-sounding car horn beeped outside the front of the house. As he shut the door behind him, he suddenly wondered where Dillon had got to.

Martha chatted nervously as she navigated through London more skilfully than a seasoned black-cab driver, taking streets that Ted never even knew existed; it was as if they opened up just to let Martha through and then closed quietly behind them. Ted was impressed; he thought he knew London well but not compared to her.

He watched Martha as she talked, her full lips moving so fast it was hard to tell they were moving at all. Her green eyes darted between mirrors, not missing a thing, hands flicking the indicators as she turned the wheel with speed and accuracy. Ted was entranced.

'…don't you think…? Ted?'

'Eh?'

'Don't you think we should start at the scene of the accident and work backwards across the park?'

'Er, yes, good idea,' Ted stammered, suddenly aware he'd been staring at her. He quickly looked out of the window to hide his embarrassment.

They had already reached the Stoke Newington area and Martha appeared to be looking for a parking space. She found one and expertly reverse-parked into a space that Ted was sure the car would never fit. As they got out, Ted felt his pocket vibrate; it was his dad. He answered his phone, quickly apologising for the strange call he'd made earlier. He explained what had happened and that he and Martha were at the scene of the accident now and were having a look around.

'But the police have already done that, Ted. What are you expecting to find?'

'I don't know, Dad, but it's like you said, it's better to be doing something, and you never know, they might have missed something,' Ted insisted.

There was silence on the end of the phone.

'Dad?'

'I'm nodding.'

'OK, well I'll keep you posted. Speak later.'

As Ted hung up the phone he realised his dad hadn't asked anything more about Martha, or what he'd been doing for the last week. Nor did he seem that bothered by their last phone call. His dad's usual interest and optimism was lacking and Ted feared he was losing hope.

He looked around for Martha and spotted her further up the road and jogged to catch up with her.

'Everything alright?' she asked absently, looking around her like a true investigative journalist.

'Yes, just Dillon calling to see where I am.' As he heard the lie come out of his mouth, he wondered for the second time that day where the hell Dillon was. He felt resentful that he wasn't here with him helping to look. After all, he was his best friend.

'There's the entrance to the park, directly opposite,' said Martha, indicating towards the gateway. 'She would have seen the road and all the cars before she got here so it must have been intentional that she threw herself into the road. What I don't understand is why she wasn't hit; it's such a busy road.

'Although,' she said, looking at the road again, 'there is a pedestrian crossing just there so perhaps the traffic was stationary right at the time she ran into the road.' This was said more to herself than Ted. 'But that wouldn't account for why nobody seemed to notice that she was being chased.'

Ted was beginning to wonder if his presence was necessary.

'Perhaps no one cares,' said Ted under his breath.

Martha frowned but ignored him.

'I suggest we take the most direct route across the park and see what's on the other side.'

Ted nodded and followed her over the road and across the park. They walked past a fountain, scattering pigeons, and it was unsettling to think of Rosie running this exact same path not long ago.

'She would have run to the nearest exit, not wanting to get lost or be too far away from public places or people,' Martha commentated as she walked. Ted tried to follow her train of thought, though the logic was baffling him slightly. He'd never been into detective stories; things were either there or they weren't as far as he was concerned, but Martha seemed like she'd just stepped out of one, appearing to love the intrigue and the mystery. In fact, now that Ted was thinking about it, she bore an uncanny resemblance to Rosie in that respect. No wonder she could think like her.

They walked past an aviary with colourful birds that looked strangely out of place, then over a bridge and out through the gate that Martha thought Rosie must have entered the park by. They stood looking around them. Ted pretended to be pondering which way to go but really he had no clue and was waiting for Martha to take the lead. He watched her eyes scan the street as if she was seeing something he wasn't privy to.

'I think left. I don't think she would have run up the road and then doubled back through the park, she would have run in a straight line away from where she was being kept,' Martha said decisively.

'I was thinking the same,' agreed Ted.

Martha flashed him a knowing smile. 'Great minds…'

They walked past small shops, cafes, restaurants, Martha looking in all the windows, as well as studying the streets and their signs.

'What are you looking for, exactly?' asked Ted, thinking that she was going slightly over the top and fancied herself as a young Miss Marple.

'I'm just keeping my eyes open and making sure I take everything in. You never know what might present itself.'

Ted stifled a snigger as he wandered on past her, deciding to take in the bigger picture and look up and around him more. Turned out it was just more of the same; more bars, more shops, nothing that looked like somewhere child traffickers would be keeping innocent, defenceless kids.

'I'm gonna grab a drink, want anything?' he heard Martha shout from a few feet behind him.

He nodded and headed back towards her as she popped into a café. As he passed the window he looked inside where something caught his eye. Leant up against the window was a photograph that looked weirdly familiar. He pressed his face against the glass. It was him! Pushing past Martha and sending cutlery flying, he reached behind a plant and pulled out the photograph.

'Ted, what the hell are you doing?'

'Rosie,' he whispered, staring at the picture.

'What?'

'This picture. It's me!'

'Don't be daft, of course it's not you, that's a kid with a seagull on his head,' said Martha, looking over his shoulder. 'And his name's Cliff, not Ted.'

'Funny. It *is* me!'

Ted rushed over to the waitress.

'Excuse me, have you had a girl in here recently? Umm, yesterday it must have been. Blonde hair, longish?'

Ted remembered the photo he had of Rosie and pulled it out to show the waitress.

'Yeah, she was in here yesterday with a strange bloke, tried to leave without paying.'

'Did you see which direction she ran in?' asked Ted excitedly.

'Er, yeah, she went out the door and left, I think. Why, do you know her? You gonna pay her debt?'

Ted looked distractedly towards the door.

'Er, sure, here.' He threw a tenner at the startled waitress and walked back to Martha.

'Rosie must have left this picture. She took it from me the day she was caught, she must have found it in her pocket and worked out a way to leave it as a clue,' Ted said excitedly.

Martha took the picture and studied it.

'Cute.'

Ted blushed.

'Wait a minute, what's this scratched at the bottom? Looks like the number fifty-five.'

Ted grabbed the picture back. 'What do you think it means?'

'Perhaps it's where they're keeping her,' suggested Martha.

'Excuse me. Do you live around here?' Ted asked the waitress.

'Yeah, not far.'

'Do you know if there is a number fifty-five on this street?'

The waitress looked out of the window.

'Umm, yeah there is, and there's also a few tower blocks that may go up that high. Do you have the address there?'

But Ted was already heading out the door, dragging Martha behind him.

# Chapter 19

It was still dark when Rosie was awoken by the sound of someone entering the room. She held her breath, frozen with fear, praying it wasn't the creepy man here to help himself to his new purchase. She feigned sleep from under the blanket and hoped it was just the girls back from their engagements. Rosie heard whoever it was creeping around the room, opening drawers and then finally the rustling of sheets as they got into one of the beds. It sounded like only one person rather than two.

'You awake?' she heard a whisper from the darkness.

Rosie turned over and blinked into the dim orange glow from the lights outside. 'Yes,' she replied.

'Thought so.' Rosie could hear a smile in the voice. 'We pretend to be asleep all the time when Silas creeps in and tries to help himself.'

Rosie shivered, she was glad it hadn't been Silas this time.

'My name's Mai-Li, what's yours?' she asked.

'Rosie.'

'Rosie… Rosie…' said Mai-Li, turning it over in her mouth. 'I think I've heard that name somewhere before,' she said dreamily.

And then all was silent and Rosie guessed Mai-Li had fallen asleep.

Rosie lay awake for a while, happy that a kind voice had spoken to her from the darkness. It had taken her ages to get to sleep before, she'd felt so homesick, not only for her family but for Baduwa, Utibe and Lo. She wondered what they were doing and hoped they were giving each other comfort. Longing for Lo's warm little body next to her, she realised how much reassurance and comfort he had provided for her, just with his silent presence; probably more than she had ever given him. He had become a security blanket for her, a favourite teddy, and she felt lost and lonely without him.

As Rosie was drifting off to the one place she felt safe, the door creaked open. Holding her breath, she prayed it was the other girls returning but the footsteps didn't sound like those with heels, they were sturdy, heavy soled. Nearer and nearer they came, until Rosie could hear panting and smell onions and beer. She tried to relax and regulate her own breathing, remembering what Mai-Li had said about pretending to be asleep, but it felt like forever that he just stood there, watching her. Suddenly he leaned forward, his breath moving her hair as he inhaled deeply and Rosie willed the mattress to swallow her up. There was a tug on the blanket that was wrapped tightly around Rosie and she gripped one side while he pulled urgently on the other. He tugged some more, this time harder and Rosie could feel it begin to slip from her hand; panic rising in her chest, she waited for him to crawl into bed beside her.

But to Rosie's surprise he suddenly let go, his footsteps receding before a soft click of the door told her he was gone. Rosie was confused but hugely relieved as she lay there gasping, her heart racing, pulling the blanket tighter around herself as she lay curled in the darkness. There was no way she'd be able to sleep now.

***

As Rosie slowly opened her eyes, she saw a young girl so beautiful and delicate that it almost took her breath away. She was brushing her waist-length, silky hair and in the brightness it looked almost ethereal. Rosie thought she must still be asleep when the girl suddenly giggled and Rosie realised she had been staring at Mai-Li.

'Sorry,' said Rosie, shyly. 'I was just admiring your hair.' Rosie ran her hand through her own mop apologetically and shrugged. Mai-Li giggled some more.

'Hungry?' she asked, putting her brush down and heading for the door.

Rosie watched fascinated as Mai-Li expertly handled the meagre food ingredients they had, and managed to produce an omelette fit for a queen. Rosie ate it hungrily, not realising how famished she'd actually been; the warmth and vitality flooding her body with every mouthful.

It wasn't until Rosie had finished every last scrap on her plate that she looked up and saw Mai-Li eating in the same ravenous fashion. No polite chit-chat, no chewing each mouthful several times to aid digestion; this was animalistic, survival of the fittest, eat or be eaten behaviour. And Rosie realised how much she'd changed in such a short time; she was integrating, adapting, soon she would be one of them, her past life just a dream she'd once had.

Suddenly the door creaked and swung open and Rosie jumped up out of her seat. She was surprised and embarrassed by her unexpected reaction and sat down quickly as the other two girls walked through the door. They looked at Rosie as they passed the doorway but neither smiled or acknowledged her presence.

'Don't mind them,' said Mai-Li, smiling. 'They're not very friendly. They're what's known in the business as a Gemini. They come as a pair, are engaged as a pair, and they are each made to play a part. It makes them very introverted; they only really communicate with each other. They're kind of like twins, I guess.'

'Where are they from?' asked Rosie.

'I think they're both from Norway but they didn't know each other before they were caught. They were just put together coz they can speak the same language and they look similar, I guess.'

Rosie didn't think they looked at all alike but she didn't want to contradict the one friend she had made.

They sat in silence for a while; Rosie could feel Mai-Li studying her.

'Silas came into our room last night, didn't he?' she suddenly said.

Rosie looked at her in surprise. 'You heard him?'

Mai-Li smiled. 'No, I could tell from the way you jumped when the door opened just now. Did he do anything?'

Rosie shook her head. 'That's what was weird; he stood over me, sniffed me, and tried to tug my blanket off but he didn't force himself on me.'

'He's a complete coward that's why; luckily for us. He's as mean as anything the rest of the time but when it comes to getting something from us himself, physically, he can't do it. I don't think it's coz he's got a kind bone in his body, it's that he's insecure in his sexuality.' Mai-Li scoffed. 'I think he sits in his flat thinking about us, talking himself into how he's all that, and then comes to our room and bottles it. He must have a teeny weeny!' Mai-Li giggled.

The other girls came in and looked at Rosie and Mai-Li in disgust as they helped themselves to some food, whispering to each other as their tall, willowy white bodies glided around the room.

'Hi, girls, good night?' asked Mai-Li in a loud, provocative voice. She winked at Rosie as they scowled in her direction and left the room with their food.

'How do you stay so happy and upbeat?' Rosie didn't want to sound mean but she was surprised at how positive Mai-Li was when there was nothing in their situation that could be worth smiling about.

Mai-Li looked taken aback.

'I don't know what you mean, I'm not happy, not at all. In fact, I'm miserable most of the time. I guess I'm just pleased that you're here and you don't ignore me. And this place is a million times better than any of the other places I've been. Silas is a pig but nothing compared to some of the men I've known, plus I now have a few regulars that are OK to me. I've been in this a long time, I've forgotten what it's like to have a normal life, so when I find myself in a place that is a little less awful than the last, I figure I should be grateful.'

'How long have you been here?' asked Rosie, suddenly feeling guilty.

'Well, my father sold me when I was about three, I think. There was me and four sisters – three of us were sold abroad and the other two kept at home to look after him and our mother. I was the youngest and was with my sisters for a while but they soon split us up and sold us on. I haven't seen or heard from them in about eight years.'

'I'm sorry,' whispered Rosie, yet again realising how lucky she was to have a family that didn't feel the need to sell her.

'How did you get mixed up in all this?' asked Mai-Li.

Rosie told the story of how she was caught at the beach, thrown in a truck with loads of other kids and brought to London. She spoke fondly of Baduwa, Utibe and Lo who she'd left behind, and of her escape attempt. She also mentioned The Lock, at which Mai-Li jumped out of her chair.

'I knew it! I thought I recognised you. I've been sitting here trying to work out what's so familiar about you. Do you sometimes wear a wig?' Mai-Li asked excitedly.

Rosie nodded. 'Only when I went to The Lock or on engagements.'

'I saw you then, at The Lock. And oh!' She jumped around more excitedly. 'Someone was looking for you; big fat bloke, balding, bad breath, except that it wasn't Mr Hungerford it was your brother Ted!' By now Mai-Li was skipping around the room like a mad thing and Rosie was struggling to keep up.

'I don't understand,' said Rosie. 'My brother's not big and fat.'

'No, no, he was in a disguise! He had somehow managed to get into The Lock disguised as one of the regulars who happens to be one of my regulars. Such a small world! Don't ask me how because he was completely out of his depth, it seemed, but he managed to engage me… not that we actually did anything… no, far too much of a gent, but we hung out together for a few days to keep his cover up whilst he waited for you to turn up.'

Rosie's head was spinning by the time Mai-Li took a breath and sat down again.

'It was great for me coz I could just sleep and hang out in the hotel room without any of the nasty stuff. And your brother's quite interesting.'

Rosie screwed up her nose. 'No he's not!' She suddenly laughed. It felt so amazing to know that he was actually looking and, more to the point, hadn't given up!

'How is he? Did he look OK? Not too stressed or tired?' asked Rosie, anxiously, worried that it must be at least a week ago since Mai-Li had seen Ted and maybe he had given up by now.

'Well I couldn't see his real face could I, silly? But he seemed OK. He was more upbeat when I first met him than at the end of the week when there hadn't been any sign of you.'

'Had you seen me before my brother turned up?' asked Rosie.

'Yeah, with two black girls, who I guess were Baduwa and Utibe?' Mai-Li replied. 'I assumed it must have been one of your first times coz you didn't look like you knew what was going on.' She giggled.

'I didn't, I was crapping myself,' replied Rosie. 'Then I got engaged by someone there and went to their house and by the time I came out I couldn't remember what had happened and I was covered in bruises and cuts all over.' Rosie shivered at the thought. 'How did Ted know where to look for me? Did he say?' asked Rosie, quickly changing the subject.

'Umm, he said you'd left him some clue which had led him to London and then the police had suggested that you might have been trafficked, and then he asked around, I think, and someone had mentioned The Lock.'

'What else did he talk about?' asked Rosie, excitedly. 'Did he mention Mum and Dad?'

'Not much. He did say they were in London too though. But enough of that! We need to find a way to get you out of here and back home!' said Mai-Li, banging her hands down on the table.

Rosie jumped to her feet and clapped her hands, caught up in the moment of hope. 'Yes! Definitely!'

Just then a key turned in the lock and Silas' head peered round the door.

'Put these on,' he said, throwing a bag in Rosie's direction. 'We're leaving in ten.'

# Chapter 20

As Ted wandered the streets with Martha, looking for number fifty-five, he realised that if it hadn't been for Martha he never would have walked back to that café and seen the photograph. He'd been too busy scoffing at her obsessive methods and had walked straight past the window. He could have missed this chance to find his sister all because of his arrogance. He wanted to punch himself and give Martha a huge hug in gratitude but felt too shy and thought she'd probably slap him for being too friendly anyway, so he made a mental note to be really grateful once they found Rosie.

They found a number fifty-five and an old lady answered the door clothed in a large pink dress and green wellies – not the typical outfit for a trafficker, Ted figured, but each to their own. Clearly thinking Ted was her gardener she told him it was not his usual day to call and to come back when it was. Ted stifled a laugh and asked her if there was any other number fifty-fives in the area. The old woman looked at him pityingly and then directed them towards a block of flats in the opposite direction. Ted didn't have any grandparents that were still alive so wasn't sure what the correct way to deal with eccentric old people was, but he politely thanked her and promised to return to do her garden another day.

'Should have driven the car up here,' said Martha as they walked down the same stretch of road for the third time.

'Where did she say it was?' asked Ted, looking around him. 'Are you sure we haven't passed it already?'

'Don't think so. She did say it was set back off the road a bit. It can't be far from the café we were at earlier. Rosie had to have been able to see the café from where she was to know that she could leave the photo there,' Martha muttered.

'Eh?' Ted chuckled, still amused by the old lady.

Martha stopped in front of the café and looked over the road. Ted pulled up alongside and looked in the same direction. There it was, a block of flats set back from the road with hidden access in through the back. It seemed a likely place as any for traffickers to operate from, and Ted had completely missed it the first time. He hated himself for being so blind, and wondered what the hell else he'd missed.

There was a large metal gate set in a wall that enclosed what looked like the rear entrance to the flats. The gate was padlocked so they walked around in an attempt to access the building from a different side. Finding another entrance, they climbed tentatively up some stairs, unsure of what to expect, Ted again wondering if he was walking a path already trodden by Rosie. It was like she had dropped bits of herself along the way and it was still clinging to places she'd been; he could almost feel it hanging there like cobwebs.

They stood outside number fifty-five, each waiting for the other to make the first move. Ted leant forward and knocked. There was no answer. Ted knocked again, louder. Gradually the door opened and an eye peeped through the crack. Both Ted and Martha stood back, not sure what to expect, but the eye looked afraid rather than threatening, and Martha stepped forward to introduce herself. The eye darted from Martha to Ted, and back again, and when Martha mentioned Rosie's name the eye looked down.

'Look, if you know where my sister is you better say now or I'm gonna smash down the door and then beat it out of you!' shouted Ted.

Martha looked up at him in surprise, then tried to recover the situation as the door started to close. 'Look, please let us in, we just want to talk. My friend won't do anything; I won't let him. He's just desperate to find his little sister.'

But Ted couldn't stand it, he was sick of tiptoeing around everyone, and everything was suddenly taking far too long; he could almost feel Rosie nearby. So barging past Martha he forced the door open, sending the man flying backwards against the wall. As the man fell, his legs landed in front of Ted's so that he had to jump to clear them. Ted noticed that on his large, flailing feet were a pair of mustard-coloured cowboy boots. Not from around here, he decided.

He heard Martha's gasp of horror behind him as he marched along the corridor and charged through the first door he came to. It was a small kitchen, empty except for old pizza boxes and takeaway cartons. He moved on to the next door; it was locked. He stood back and threw his weight against it, not waiting for it to be opened for him. He felt unstoppable as if his mind and body had been taken over and were being controlled remotely. A vile smell hit him like a wall; a mixture of rotting food and stale air laced with despair took his breath away. Scattered over the floor were four mattresses, some ragged blankets and a few clothes. A tray of old food was festering in the corner, and huddled on the opposite side of the room, fear colouring his eyes black, was a small boy.

Ted felt Martha run into him and he barely spoke louder than a whisper, through teeth that refused to unclench, 'Call the police.'

He then turned to speak to the man but he was gone.

Ted roared through the house like a tornado, throwing open all the doors and calling Rosie's name, but the place was empty. Suddenly there was a shout from Martha. Ted followed her voice and found her holding the boy who was struggling in her arms.

'He got upset when you started shouting, I don't think he speaks much English.'

The boy was squeaking in her arms and Martha spoke in a gentle, soothing voice as she tried to calm him.

'I know Rosie was here, I can feel her. Where can she be now?' said Ted desperately.

The boy started struggling again, and then he spoke.

'Worsie.'

It was a strange pronunciation but it was definitely her name. Ted knelt down opposite him.

'Did... you... say... Rosie?' he asked slowly.

The boy nodded.

'She here?'

The boy shook his head.

'Gone,' said the boy.

'Where?' asked Ted.

But the boy just shook his head and started crying.

By the time the police arrived, Ted was sitting with his head in his hands, chastising himself for losing it and letting the man get away. They now had a boy who could barely speak English and was probably too traumatised to communicate with anyone anyway, and an empty flat with no clues as to where Rosie had been taken. The police seemed unamused at Ted's gung-ho approach and scolded him for not calling them first. Ted wanted to say that at least he was actively doing something instead of procrastinating like they had been, but thought getting himself arrested was not in Rosie's best interest.

Martha came over and sat next to Ted on the steps.

'I've given the police a description of the man, and they've handed the boy over to social services where they hope to get some information out of him. I don't fancy their chances; the kid's a complete mess. Forensics are in there now, hopefully they'll let us know if they come up with anything concrete.'

Ted shrugged. 'Sure they will. So we're back where we started then?'

'Not necessarily, the cops may come up with something. They think there have been other children here, and that there are likely to be more men involved, especially as the one we saw didn't seem quite all there,' Martha said, tapping her forehead.

'I can't believe I let him go! I was just so sure Rosie was there that she was my only thought. And I figured once we had her she could tell us about the men who had captured her and they would be found. I'm such an idiot!'

Martha put her hand gently on his knee and Ted felt tears sting the backs of his eyes.

'You can't blame yourself; you're doing the best you can. You're doing more than most brothers would. The police have a description of the man that was here and he's quite unusual-looking too, so he won't be too hard to trace, I'm sure.'

Ted jumped up and leant over the balcony. Martha's kind and reassuring words were making him want to blub and he had to get a grip. He looked down at the empty car park and watched a group of teenagers walk across it, laughing and jostling each other. It felt so long ago that he had been like that with his mates. In fact, he hadn't heard from Midge and Plank in ages. They'd deserted long before Dillon had. Ted was amazed at how easily people gave up.

Martha was at his side again, leaning into him reassuringly. Her hand found his and squeezed it. Ted looked down into her concerned green eyes and found himself leaning down and resting his forehead on hers. All the anguish and pain he'd felt seemed to seep from him down into her, and for a moment it felt like everything was right with the world.

Suddenly, out of the corner of his eye, Ted saw a car pull up on the other side of the metal gate. He slowly lifted his heavy, pounding head to see who it could be, but no one got out. Then there was a screeching of tyres and the car reversed fast and then sped away.

'That was them! It must have been,' said Ted, pointing to where the car had left smoke in its wake. 'Quick, get the nearest cop,' he said to Martha, as he leant over to see which direction it was going in.

He relayed what he'd seen to the policeman; the colour of the car and the make he thought it was, as well as the direction it was headed. The officer got on the radio straight away and rallied all available cars.

'They must have seen the police cars, and us up here,' Ted said to Martha, excitedly.

Martha nodded, grinning. 'See, there's still hope.'

Just then Ted heard the familiar voices of his parents and suddenly they were standing in front of him, and it was so good to see them. Ted flung his arms around them both.

'The police called us,' said his mum, in what sounded like a slightly accusatory tone.

'Sorry,' said Ted. It had crossed his mind to call them but he'd felt so ashamed that he'd let the man – not to mention Rosie – slip through his fingers because of his temper, that he hadn't wanted to be the one to tell them.

Ted hurriedly introduced his parents to Martha in an attempt to change the subject, and they thanked her profusely for all she'd done so far. No mention was made of the mistaken identity saga, although Martha seemed apologetic in her acceptance of their praise.

After his parents had been briefed by the police, they were told they could all leave, so Ted suggested the four of them get a drink before heading home. Ted watched Martha and his mum chatting like old friends, his dad raising an eyebrow whenever Martha put a gesturing hand on Ted as she told them the story of how they'd discovered the flat. It was strange having a girl there that wasn't Rosie, it made Ted check himself every time he started to relax into it. It almost felt like old times with them all laughing together, and although Ted felt guilty, like he was betraying Rosie, it was good to laugh. And Martha was so great with his mum and dad: funny, intelligent, reassuring, and Ted couldn't seem to look anywhere else but at her infectious smile and her long delicate fingers as they rested on his arm. He barely even heard what she said but it must have been amusing, as his face began to ache from the ridiculous grin that had made its home there.

There was much hugging and a few tears from his mum when they parted company a short time later. And as Ted and Martha walked back through the park to the car, Martha was full of praise for his parents' courage and said she hoped to be as strong and amazing a parent as they seemed one day.

'You want kids then?' asked Ted.

'Of course, don't you?'

'I don't know anymore. I mean; is it fair to bring children into this world the state it's in? How does a parent cope with knowing their child is suffering like Rosie is right now? Why would you want to risk exposing a child to that? It could happen to anyone, right? If it happened to Rosie in the one of the remotest places in the country.'

Martha stopped beside him and Ted turned to face her.

'But if everyone had that attitude no one would have kids and the human race would die out.'

'Well, would that be such a bad thing? It seems we aren't doing a very good job if we let our own children be raped, beaten, hurt…' Ted slumped down on a bench.

Martha's phone rang.

Ted looked across the walkway to the aviary. The birds seemed very quiet; there was no flapping or squawking. Ted strained to see if they were eating or asleep but they all seemed to be sitting on their perches looking in the same direction. Ted saw movement behind one of the cages and realised a man was sitting on the ground looking up at the birds. He was part hidden but Ted could see his mouth moving like he was talking to someone: the birds? One of the parrots seemed particularly interested in the man; it was sitting right in front of him its head cocked to one side as if listening intently to whatever he was saying.

Ted nudged Martha to point out this strange spectacle but she was too engrossed in her phone call and flicked him away. Ted continued to watch the strange bird-man's mouth move, and then something caught his attention: his shoes. Ted could see them under the wire; they were yellow cowboy boots. Where had he seen boots like that recently?

Then it hit him, he jumped to his feet but Martha grabbed his arm.

'Wait!' she hissed. 'I've seen him too but don't go charging over there, you'll only scare him off.'

Ted pulled out his phone. She was right, he didn't want another bollocking from the police for trying to handle things on his own.

'Don't!' said Martha, grabbing his phone. 'What are you doing?'

'We have to call the police.'

'No, we'll lose him, maybe for good. If he refuses to talk to the police and they don't have enough evidence to hold him, he'll disappear and we'll lose the one chance we have to find Rosie.'

Ted sat back down but made sure not to take his eyes off the man; there was no way he was losing him again. 'What do you suggest then?'

'I'll go talk to him; I can be very persuasive when I want to.'

Ted looked at her doubtfully. 'I don't know. He's a dangerous man, Martha. Who knows what he's really capable of?'

'I can do this, Ted. Trust me.'

Ted looked up into her pleading eyes and shrugged. 'OK, but I'll be straight on him if he makes one move, OK?'

'Sure, but otherwise stay away until I give you the signal. He'll bolt like a rabbit if he feels threatened and then we're back to nowhere again.'

Ted watched anxiously as Martha walked over to the man and sat down on the ground next to him. They seemed to talk for ages as Ted stared unblinking, afraid of missing Martha's signal. He was finding it very frustrating not being able to hear what they were saying but Martha seemed to have it under control so Ted relaxed his guard a little.

It was starting to get late and people were rushing past, anxious to get home. Just as Ted was beginning to think he'd have to make a bed on the bench where he sat, Martha got up and walked towards him. He stood, nervous that she'd left the man's side and may risk letting him get away again, but Martha shook her head as if to say *it's OK*. As she drew closer Ted studied her expression to get a heads up on the situation before she reached him but her face gave nothing away.

'Griff's agreed to take me to where Rosie is but only if I go alone and you stay away. He says he doesn't want to risk being caught and he thinks if you're there you'll turn him in once he's given us Rosie.'

Martha didn't look him in the eye as she was talking and Ted couldn't work out if she was uncomfortable with the situation but felt she had to go along with it, or wasn't telling him the whole truth.

'No way, you're not going anywhere with him on your own,' replied Ted. 'Let me at him, he'll soon tell us what he knows,' he said angrily, trying to push past Martha.

She grabbed his arm. 'Don't be an idiot!' she hissed. 'This could be our one chance to find Rosie and you're not messing it up with your macho bullshit!'

Ted stepped back, wounded. He'd never heard Martha talk like that before and it was like hearing a stranger speak.

'I don't trust him,' said Ted quietly, feeling like a naughty puppy that had just been scolded for peeing on the floor.

Martha softened and touched his arm as she said, 'I'll be fine, he's harmless, wouldn't say boo to a badger. Go home, I'll call you as soon as I have Rosie.'

She was so calm, as if she was just going somewhere with an old friend, rather than a strange man that had kidnapped Rosie and done goodness knows what else to her. And as the pair left the park, something felt very wrong, but Ted couldn't put his finger on it. He remembered from earlier at the flat that Griff had seemed childlike, infantile, like there was something wrong with him, and he hadn't put up any resistance when Ted barged in. But there was something about the way he was walking beside Martha, and he hadn't looked at Ted once the whole time he'd been talking to her, like he'd already known he was there.

Ted's blood was beginning to run cold; he'd been here before, in a similar situation when he'd let Rosie go off, and had made the wrong decision then too. He couldn't risk it happening again. He stood up, and, staying in the shadows, followed Martha and Griff out of the park.

# Chapter 21

The clothes Rosie was now shivering in were similar to the ones she'd worn the other times; designed to show enough of her to tantalise but not to give everything away. She guessed this new guy, Silas, must be a little further down the food chain than Zaydain and Gabriel because the new club she was standing outside was more neon and nicotine stains than strobes and champagne. As they entered the dingy club, weaselly, spineless little men, much like Silas, were all leaning and leering in the semi-darkness.

Silas bought Rosie a drink, said it was to loosen her up and that there was nothing worse for a man than a stiff, frigid, whimpering girl. She gratefully downed it, not caring what his reasons were, gasping as it caught in her throat and then savouring the warmth as it filled her body. It was so reassuring that she almost felt comfortable in her sordid surroundings and suddenly the tiny weaselly men weren't so scary after all, they were soft, edgeless creatures that swirled and slithered as they tried to get the best angle on the girls. Rosie found herself smiling, this wasn't so bad after all, maybe she was starting to get used to it.

The music seemed to get louder and Rosie felt herself start to sway to its provocative beat. She discarded her coat and hugged her body as it moved, enjoying the attention from the many eyes that had turned her way. Rosie knew Silas had given her more than just alcohol but she didn't care, this was the best feeling ever, and as she watched Silas talking to the men, she was surprised to find herself liking the way he looked, thinking there was actually something very desirable about him. In fact, all the men around her were handsome in their own way, and she could tell from their eyes they all wanted her too. She danced more vigorously, wanting to give them a show, but Silas seemed to get protective of her suddenly and insisted she put her coat back on.

'We're not handing out free shows here,' he hissed in her ear. 'Save yourself for the ones who put their money where their mouth is.'

Rosie was plied with more drinks and sent to a private room with mirrors and low lighting. The sofa felt comfortable beneath her as she lay down, giggling as she caught sight of her reflection in the mirror on the ceiling. She had never seen such a large image of herself in so few clothes, and as she studied her reflection she was shocked by how much her hair had grown and how much older she looked.

The little room soon became popular, men coming and going, some for a kiss and a grope, others staying longer. But Rosie was unsure of the time, her eyes refusing to stay open, as each face merged into one. All she could hear were distant, echoing voices in her ears as if she were under water; her head bobbing dizzily on the surface, before sinking down and down into the murky blackness where all was quiet, then rising slowly again, the voices and music becoming louder until all she could hear was heavy breathing and grunting.

Rosie rode this wave of uncertainty and confusion for what felt like hours. Sometimes she tried to sit up but something heavy was always pushing her down.

Suddenly she vomited. She heard a man's voice swearing somewhere nearby. Then Silas was there, standing over her, pulling at her arms that refused to bring her body with them. He seemed to be shouting but Rosie couldn't understand why. Her mouth tasted horrible and she asked for a drink, but Silas pulled her to her feet and she staggered out of the room, past the bar and out into the cold night air. She felt sure it had been daylight when she'd gone into the club. How long had she been in there?

***

Rosie awoke to the familiar orange glow from the streetlights. She tried to move but her body screamed out in pain. What had happened to her? She called out, 'Mai-Li!' And, as if by magic, Mai-Li was at her side.

'It's OK, you're safe now,' came Mai-Li's soothing voice.

Rosie felt something cool on her forehead and then nothing.

When she awoke again the light from the windows pierced her eyes like red-hot pokers. Her head pounded, her body ached. She could hear crying next to her. She reached out her hand towards the sound and someone took hold and squeezed.

'It's OK, I'm fine,' Rosie heard herself say. 'Don't cry.'

'Sorry, it's just that it's almost worse when you see someone else after engagements coz you realise that's what you look like.'

'Oh, thanks!' said Rosie, attempting a smile. 'Do I look that bad?'

'Well, to be honest, you did look better before you left. But it's nothing that won't heal, on the outside anyway.'

'I don't really remember what happened though, so maybe that's a good thing,' said Rosie, creasing her forehead as she tried to recall the last twenty-four hours.

'That's the one good thing about Silas, he likes his women soft and agreeable, not stiff and reluctant, so he slips what he calls *looseners* into the drinks he gives you,' said Mai-Li. 'It means you're so out of it you rarely remember or feel a thing, until afterwards that is. It often comes back in nightmares, but you can leave it there, in your dreams, if you keep really busy while you're awake.'

'He definitely drugged me,' said Rosie, recognising the familiar feeling of a comedown.

'Believe me, it's the best way to go. You don't want to be alert at any stage of the engagements,' said Mai-Li, sniffing and wiping her nose on her arm. 'Remember you asked me how come I'm so happy a lot of the time considering what's happened to me?'

Rosie nodded.

'Well, mostly it's because I rarely remember anything. My mind has been so messed up by Silas' shit that I can barely remember my family or my home anymore.'

Rosie thought of her own home but it looked different now, smaller, further away. In the beginning it was where she longed to be more than any other place on earth, but now she felt a bit like Mai-Li, like she couldn't remember what she had been missing. She wasn't sure what had suddenly changed or whether it was something that had been happening slowly over time, but the longing she had felt to be home with her family was dying, and memories of her life before all this were starting to fade. She feared that if someone didn't find her soon there would be nothing left of her but an empty, lifeless shell.

Rosie tried to swing her legs out of the bed but they felt so heavy. She leant up on one elbow and tried to stop the room spinning. Her mouth felt like old carpet as she reached for the water that Mai-Li had put by the bed.

'You hungry?' asked Mai-Li, taking the glass off Rosie as she was trying to put it back on the table. Rosie shook her head, the thought of food made her head spin more and her supporting arm gave way, dropping her back on the bed.

'I'm gonna make something anyway so I'll make extra for you in case you feel hungry later,' said Mai-Li, bustling out of the room.

Rosie wondered how someone who couldn't be more than thirteen or fourteen could be so mature beyond her years. She had just reminded Rosie so much of her mum that her heart lurched at the thought and tears poured uncontrollably from her eyes. The numbness she'd woken up to was beginning to subside and unimaginable sadness was trying to take its place.

Rosie tried to stand again. She couldn't just lie there thinking, it was likely to send her insane. Like Mai-Li said; best to keep busy. She looked out through the barred window for the first time, cars flashed in the sunlight as they passed on the other side of the trees. Rosie felt so jealous of those cars and the people in them; even the most mundane desperate life had to be better than the one she was living now.

'There's no way out, believe me, I've tried,' said Mai-Li as she entered the room. She was carrying a plate of toast and two cups of tea, and Rosie sat down, finally submitting to the hunger that had been lying dormant in her stomach.

'How long have you been here?' asked Rosie, working a piece of toast around her dry, sore mouth.

Mai-Li looked up at the ceiling in contemplation. 'Um, not sure, you lose track of time, yer know? Maybe a year, might even be two.'

Rosie felt ill at the thought of such a long time in a place like this. She couldn't get her head around how Mai-Li remained so seemingly normal under such circumstances. Could it really be a lifestyle that you could get used to in time? Surely the body and mind had limits to such abuse.

The lock turned in the door and one of the Norwegian girls walked in. Her face was red and blotchy, there was blood on her top lip, and she had bruises up her arms.

Rosie looked at Mai-Li questioningly but she just shrugged. They both sat watching, waiting for an explanation but the girl merely lay on her bed shivering uncontrollably.

Rosie got up, wincing from the pain, and went over to her.

'Are you OK?' she asked quietly.

Mai-Li came and sat on the floor beside the bed.

'What happened, Jelena?'

It seemed like she couldn't speak; her teeth were chattering and her breathing was erratic.

'Shh,' soothed Mai-Li. 'Try to relax your body and slow your breathing, you're hyperventilating.'

Jelena shook her head, burying her face in her pillow, where she let out a scream that ripped through Rosie and tore at her very being. Tears immediately sprang into her own eyes.

Jelena sobbed and sobbed until she was a broken, sodden rag doll of a person, whilst Rosie and Mai-Li sat solemnly by the bed stroking her gently. When it seemed like Jelena could not possibly have any sadness left in her she stopped crying and lay staring empty-eyed. Rosie and Mai-Li looked at each other, neither knowing what to do, so they got up and tiptoed out of the room hoping Jelena would sleep for a while.

'What could have happened?' Rosie asked Mai-Li when they'd shut the door to the kitchen.

'The worst.'

'What's the worst?'

'Well, do you see Tihana anywhere?'

'You mean...?'

Mai-Li nodded.

'Does that really happen?' Rosie asked, somewhat sceptically.

Mai-Li let out a burst of laughter that was devoid of humour.

'It's nearly happened to me several times, and if you're here for long enough it could easily happen to you too.'

Mai-Li seemed almost angry with her, and Rosie felt like a small naïve child.

'But I didn't know…' whispered Rosie.

Rosie suddenly became aware that Jelena was standing in the doorway. Her face was ashen; she looked like a walking corpse. Mai-Li went over to her and guided her gently to a seat. Her bruises looked angry and her lip had swollen to match her puffy red eyes.

Mai-Li busied herself making tea, so all Rosie could do was sit next to Jelena and feel awkward. Jelena seemed unable to sit still; she picked at her nails, pulled at her hair, her eyes darting about as if seeing things that weren't there.

'It should have been me,' she whispered, stroking her bruised arms.

Rosie put her hand tentatively on Jelena's shoulder but Jelena shrank away from it. Rosie felt even more awkward and dejected as she took back her hand.

'What happened, Jelena?' said Mai-Li, setting a cup of tea down on the table.

'I can't tell you. I know not how to put in words; not English words anyway. There are no words to say what

Tihana suffered before she died… and they made me watch it all.'

She looked around as if searching for a better way to explain then picked up a knife. She engraved a round head shape on the table and then cut a smile right across the face that extended further than a normal smile would. She then placed three vertical lines leading up into it and etched below them the words 'Devil's Fork'.

'That's what they call it, the men who did this to her. They made her mouth wider to fit…'

Rosie gasped as she realised what Jelena was describing. Mai-Li shot her a look that silenced her horror. Jelena moved the blade of the knife slowly over her wrist and started to make an incision. Rosie realised what she was doing and grabbed her arm, pulling the knife from her hand. Then she was screaming again. 'There was nothing I could do to save her! They never stop… stop… cutting her!'

Rosie dropped the knife on the floor and grabbed Jelena around the arms and held on to her as she writhed and thrashed, screaming Tihana's name over and over. Rosie hugged Jelena tighter than she'd ever hugged anyone before, as if she could suffocate the pain from her body. Then suddenly Jelena slowed and stopped as if her batteries had run out. They both sank to the floor, and there they stayed, Rosie rocking her gently, until Jelena fell asleep in her arms.

# Chapter 22

What kind of a name was Griff anyway? thought Ted as he stared through the window separating his train carriage from theirs. They weren't talking anymore and Martha seemed on edge. Had she changed her mind about doing this?

Because he hadn't known where they were headed, Ted had had to get a ticket to the end of the line for the Tube and both train journeys; it had cost him a fortune and most of it was wasted as they only went a few stops each time. As they pulled into Streatham Hill station Griff ushered Martha off the train. Ted followed at a distance behind a large man devouring a bumper bag of Wotsits. It made Ted realise how hungry he was. Griff's long legs strode up the hill forcing Martha to trot comically at his side to keep up. Ted was surprised that Martha hadn't looked back, surely she would have guessed that he'd follow; although his reputation for leaving girls to fend for themselves against traffickers may have preceded him.

The big man eating crisps veered away to cross the road and Ted suddenly found himself completely exposed. He stopped and started in confusion, and then shot behind a phone box to wait until Martha and Griff had gone further up the road. He hoped no one was watching him because he thought he must look ridiculous darting about like a long-legged detective from a really old cartoon.

As they reached the brow of the hill, Griff steered Martha to the pedestrian crossing. Ted held his position until they were safely on the other side before waiting for the next green light and crossing himself.

He'd watched them turn right down Church Road, but when he got there, there was no sign of them. Ted began to run, fear gripping his chest; he couldn't have lost her, surely. He looked left across the road at the council estate with its high-rise flats huddled together like women gossiping on a street corner: nothing. He looked right at some grassy scrubland, a wall of houses flanking it. Still nothing. What if he'd lost her? he thought, as he ran helplessly left then right and back again. Then he'd officially be the worst person on the planet, and the most stupid. What idiot could lose two girls to traffickers in the space of a few weeks? There was a turning off to the right; he stopped to look down it, but no sign. He didn't know whether to keep running the way he was going or to take the road off. He hesitated, terrified of making the wrong choice. Then his phone rang.

'Ted mate, it's me,' came Dillon's nervous voice on the end.

'I can't talk now, I'm having a nightmare,' snapped Ted, hanging up his phone.

From his voice it sounded like Dillon was ringing to grovel, but Ted wasn't ready to forgive him for being a deserter, and he was angered even more by the thought that if Dillon had been with him, as he should be, they could have split up and looked in both directions and he wouldn't be standing uselessly on this corner wasting precious time with his indecisiveness. Ted held his aching head in his hands; the lack of sleep was beginning to take its toll on his nerves and he could feel himself falling apart from the inside out.

His phone rang again and he cursed at the interruption.

'Dillon, I really don't have time to talk right now,' he snarled.

'It's Dad. Is everything OK? You sound upset.'

Ted slumped down on the edge of the pavement; the sound of his dad's voice broke through his hard, angry wall and released a flood of sadness that threatened to break the surface of his eyes.

'Sorry, Dad, I'm fine, just tired. What's up?'

'Good news for a change; the police caught two men that were possibly involved in Rosie's kidnapping, probably the ones you saw racing away in that car. And there was a kid with them too, a girl. The police apparently had an anonymous tip-off giving up their number plate and car make. They were apprehended a few miles from the flat.'

'Really?' replied Ted. 'They said anything yet?'

His dad paused. 'Not much. And the girl is so traumatised she hasn't been very helpful. But the police are confident they'll get something out of someone soon. And the girl did confirm that Rosie had been with her up until a couple of days ago. Look, don't be disheartened. You and Martha are doing great. Is she there with you?'

*Afraid not Dad, I'm a useless bastard and have let her be taken by one of the traffickers because, despite it happening once before with my own sister, I appear to be incapable of recognising when not to let a girl go off with strange men!* Ted felt like saying.

'No, she's gone home for the night,' he lied instead. Again.

'Oh, well, I'll have to catch up with her tomorrow then,' his dad said, sounding so much more cheerful than in their last few conversations. 'I'll let you know if the cops call again with any news. You get some sleep OK? You must be knackered.'

Ted nodded, forgetting his dad couldn't see, and hung up the phone.

Ted looked around him again, defeated and exhausted, but he couldn't go home and leave Martha somewhere in one of these houses alone. He had to stay and at least try to find her.

He stared down at the phone in his hand; maybe he should call the police. They would be able to search all the houses around here and find Martha quicker than he could on his own. But what would they say when they found out that he had, yet again, tried to handle things on his own and lost another girl to the traffickers in the process? They'd probably lock him up for hindering an investigation or something. No, this was on him, and he would sort it, somehow.

Ted took himself back to the trees and scrubland he'd passed earlier and made a nest within view of the street. He would wait and watch for a while and see if anyone passed by that might give him a clue as to where Martha might be. He crossed his arms close to his body and sat huddled, eyes unblinking as he scrutinised each passer-by. Occasionally one would spot him and immediately cross to the other side of the street assuming he was waiting in ambush. And, yet again, Ted's perspective of the world and its workings shifted.

After a while his eyes started to flicker as he strained to keep them from closing. The cold was reaching his bones and he knew that soon he wouldn't be able to keep warm. But it was his well-deserved punishment for losing Martha, and he took it as such. She had been nothing but amazing and now she was probably no better off than Rosie. He should be more than shivering! Ted could imagine the disappointment in Martha's eyes when she realised she'd walked into a trap and that Ted was nowhere to be seen. That he'd lost her so easily, like he'd lost Rosie. And the thought of her disappointment made Ted shake uncontrollably. She would never have done anything so stupid; she would have risked more, considered the possibilities of losing them and done something about it sooner. He hated the idea that she probably thought he was a bumbling idiot, because it was slowly becoming apparent that he liked her, a lot; more than someone in a situation like this probably should. But he couldn't help it, and if he ever found her he would tell her so.

Suddenly, through the blur of his lovesick haze, Ted saw Griff and another, much bigger man. They were heading back towards the train station. Ted immediately sprang to his feet, and before he knew it was standing right in front of Griff, shouting and swearing at him. Griff immediately took steps backwards and cowered behind his arm as if Ted was about to swing at him, but the other man stepped forward and squared up to Ted.

'Move, kid, before you get yourself hurt,' said the giant.

'I won't until he tells me what he did with my friend and where my sister is!' shouted Ted, pointing at Griff.

''im?' The giant laughed, elbowing Griff so that he toppled sideways like a rag doll. 'He couldn't do anything without being told. It's me you wanna be asking.'

'OK, where are they?'

'Well that would be telling now, wouldn't it?' he sneered, pushing past.

Ted swung his fist hoping to make contact but the giant merely lifted his own tree-trunk of an arm and caught Ted's far smaller one, twisting it behind his back.

'You won't get away with this!' Ted snarled.

'Already have.'

'What's to stop me calling the cops right now and telling them what you look like and where you are?' threatened Ted.

'Nothing except that if you do, I'll be back for your parents.' The giant pulled harder on Ted's arm.

Ted gasped. His parents?

'Please,' winced Ted. 'Just let them go; they're innocent. I won't say a word to the cops if you just let me have them back.'

'Can't do that, they're worth too much to me. Turns out white girls are in huge demand and people will pay proper money for them. Zaydain was dead wrong...' he muttered, releasing Ted's arm and pushing him away. 'And once they're out of the country you won't find them or us anyway.'

Ted lunged for the giant again. 'You're not taking them anywhere!' he shouted, fear fuelling the rage.

'Not much you can do about it now is there.' The giant sniffed, flicking Ted away and pushing Griff on down the road in front of him.

'I can help,' said Ted, suddenly coming up with an idea.

'Help with what?' asked the giant, turning around.

'Help with getting you out of the country unnoticed. After all, you can't be sure that I won't tell the police what you look like, despite your threats, and there are all these witnesses passing by in their cars who have seen you,' said Ted, waving his arm towards the road. 'But I could get you a disguise, and a passport, so you could leave the country and go anywhere you liked, disappear forever.'

He had the giant's attention now, although he was eyeing Ted suspiciously.

'And what would you want in return?' he asked slowly.

'I want the girls.'

The giant thought for a moment then said, 'You can have one.'

'No way, both or no deal!'

'One is better than none.'

'I'm offering you freedom!' shouted Ted.

'A life for a life is a fair deal, take it or leave it,' said the giant, turning to leave.

'OK!' yelled Ted, realising if he lost this chance he may never see his sister again.

# Chapter 23

Rosie was emotionally drained. Jelena had been climbing the walls all day, tormenting herself over Tihana's death; she was either angry and screaming or crying and suicidal. Rosie and Mai-Li had taken it in turns to watch her every move and placate her as best they could, but neither of them knew what to do. Silas had put his head round the door when he'd heard all the noise, and Mai-Li had tried to persuade him that Jelena needed to see a doctor, but he had refused, telling them to keep her quiet, or else.

Now Jelena was lying exhausted on her bed, eyes empty and staring, her breathing shallow. She seemed to have disappeared into herself and neither Rosie nor Mai-Li could get any response out of her. Rosie was beginning to worry that they were losing her.

'We have to try and get her out of here and to a doctor, it can't be good that she's like this. At least when she was shouting and crying we knew she was alive, now she just seems like she's gone somewhere far away and we may never get her back,' Rosie whispered.

Mai-Li waved her hands in front of Jelena's eyes but she didn't even blink.

'Don't you think that maybe you and I could overpower Silas between us? He's only small,' Rosie suggested.

Mai-Li shook her head, her eyes suddenly terrified.

'Why?' Rosie asked quietly, taking hold of Mai-Li's hand.

'Because it's not worth what will happen to us if we fail.'

'What will happen?'

'There's a man, this thin awkward man, I've only seen him once and just looking at him was scary enough. He came here when Jelena and Tihana were new and difficult to control because there were two of them, and he tasered them and tortured them until they begged him to leave them alone and promised to behave. Everyone is terrified of him and what he might do to them and their families, those that have ones they care about anyway.'

As she held Mai-Li's hand Rosie noticed scars on her arms. They were thin and straight, as if done by a knife or a blade of some kind. She was about to ask Mai-Li for an explanation when a memory flicked through her mind like an old silent movie. It was of a parrot that a friend from primary school had had in her house. It was the creepiest thing Rosie had ever seen and she hated going there because she could swear it watched her every move with its evil eyes, as it stood motionless on its perch. Its body was nearly bald because it plucked its own feathers out whenever anyone went too close to the cage or tried to open the door and let him out, and its skin was raw and scarred. Rosie had run home crying to her mum the first time she had seen Captain the parrot, and her mum had said there was a name for the bird's condition: cage-bound, and it was similar to agoraphobia. Fear of the outside world due to neglect, often resulting in self-mutilation.

Just then the key turned in the lock and Silas walked in holding the arm of another girl. She was struggling and swearing at him but he pushed her through the door and slammed it. She looked older than Rosie and Mai-Li, closer to Jelena's age. Her long hair was tied back in a ponytail that swayed angrily as her green eyes scanned her surroundings and took in Rosie and Mai-Li.

'Rosie?' she said, looking from one to the other questioningly.

Rosie looked at Mai-Li and then back at the girl. 'I'm Rosie,' she said quietly.

The girl flung her arms around her and sobbed.

'Oh thank God you're here. Oh I'm so relieved!' She pulled away and studied Rosie's face more closely, then looked her up and down as if checking she was all in one piece.

Although it was nice to get a welcoming hug after so long, Rosie pulled back a little in surprise. 'Who are you?' she asked.

'Oh gosh, sorry, I'm Martha. I've been helping your brother Ted to look for you. I feel like I know you, it's so weird,' she rushed. 'Are you OK?'

Rosie nodded, then laughed with joy at the sound of her brother's name. 'You know Ted?'

Martha laughed too. 'Yes, we met coz I was doing a story on trafficking and heard about your case through my brother. I wanted to help so followed Ted around for a while and then introduced myself and we've been looking for you ever since. God, it feels like such a long time ago that this all started!'

The relief that was washing over Rosie was the best feeling she could remember ever having, she was flooded with love for her brother and his unwavering determination. But there was something wrong with this picture.

'What are you doing here, though? I was hoping Ted was going to get me out, not send more people in!' said Rosie, urgently.

Martha took a deep breath and told Rosie what had happened over the last few weeks. How she'd met Ted, how they'd heard about her being hit on the road and then rescued by her dad that wasn't her dad. How they'd followed her trail backwards and found the picture and then the flat and Griff and Lo…

'Lo? You found Lo?' Rosie interrupted.

Martha nodded. 'Yes, he's safely in the care of social services.'

Rosie was so relieved. Of all of the children she had encountered, he was the one she felt most responsible for, and knowing he was safe was nearly as amazing as being safe herself.

'And what happened with Griff? Was he OK? I felt so bad about leaving him to face Gabriel's anger after I ran away. I was really worried he would get hurt.'

Martha stared disbelievingly at Rosie. 'You were worried about him?'

'Of course, he can't help the way he is.' Rosie looked from Martha to Mai-Li who she had noticed was keeping very quiet, almost cowering on the other side of the room as far from Martha and Rosie as she could get. 'You OK, Mai-Li?' she asked, walking over to her.

Mai-Li shook her head, her eyes wide with fear. 'You know Griff? You feel sorry for him?' she asked, aghast.

Rosie noticed both girls seemed to be looking at her like she was crazy. 'Yes,' she replied, suddenly unsure of herself.

'He's the one I was telling you about!' spat Mai-Li. 'The one who we're all scared of.'

Rosie stared unblinking as she took in what Mai-Li had said. 'No!' she said, trying not to laugh.

'Yes!' shouted Mai-Li. 'The guy who keeps us all in line. The one who puts the fear of God in us.' She was looking at Rosie like she was suddenly the enemy, as if she had been on the traffickers' side all the time.

'I don't understand,' said Rosie. 'He's so harmless, weird yes, but not in that way surely?'

'That's the point, he's got some mental thing.' Mai-Li tapped her head. 'He doesn't know right from wrong, he just does whatever he's told, which means none of the others have to get their hands dirty. They can just pin it all on him, if it comes to that!'

'I don't believe it,' defended Rosie. 'Griff couldn't hurt a fly!'

'Mai-Li's right,' said Martha. 'Griff may look innocent but there's something horribly wrong with him, and not in a good way.'

'But…'

'Rosie, it was probably Griff who killed Tihana,' whispered Mai-Li.

'Why didn't you say anything to me before?' asked Rosie, accusingly.

'Well I didn't know you and Griff were best friends, did I? I didn't know you were so close!' spat Mai-Li.

Rosie felt ashamed and stupid. How had she not seen that Griff was evil? She cast her mind back to their past encounters, the times he came to visit her with chocolate and drinks, how he'd been so kind and gentle with her, how he'd willingly taken her to the café – surely if he was bad he wouldn't have let her out of the flat? Unless someone had told him to… What if Gabriel had engineered the whole thing? Her escape, her capture and her transfer to Silas' house. But why? What could they be planning?

Tears flooded her eyes in shame. She really was a naïve, stupid little girl; and clearly not as streetwise as she'd thought. From somewhere in the haze of tears and embarrassment, Rosie felt Martha put her arms around her and hold her while she wept.

'Don't beat yourself up. I believed he was nice too, at the start,' soothed Martha. 'I wouldn't have spoken to him by the aviary without Ted there if I hadn't thought he was the nervous creature he appeared to be when we saw him at the flat. I still can't get the look in his eyes out of my head; the way he turned to me when I approached him, his expression shifting from feigned surprise to a grin so evil that it would stop even the kindest heart. I knew I'd made a huge mistake by insisting Ted stay away but it was too late. He immediately threatened all your lives if I didn't go with him. I had no choice. And now poor Ted is out there probably blaming himself for letting me go and losing both of us.'

Rosie lifted her heavy head from Martha's shoulder and looked at her. She saw tears in her eyes too and realised that Martha had clearly formed a strong bond with her brother through all this. 'But why was Griff so nice to me? Why did he want me to come here? What has he got planned for me, for us?'

Martha stroked Rosie's wet cheek. 'I'm not sure, but there was another man here when we arrived, a big man, and he was talking to Griff when Silas brought me up here.'

'A big man, like really tall?' Rosie whispered, noticing Mai-Li crouched on the floor, her arms wrapped around her legs, rocking.

'Yes.'

'Must be Gabriel, what could he be doing here? I thought he'd passed me on because I was so much trouble…'

'I guess they haven't finished with you yet, which is why we have to get out of here now.'

Rosie felt a surge of excitement at those words. 'You really think we can?' she asked hopefully.

'Absolutely! We're easily a match for that sad little man, Silas,' said Martha triumphantly.

'As long as it is just him…' said Rosie.

'Well we'll just have to take that chance,' said Martha.

Rosie started looking around for anything they could use as a weapon. 'Help me, Mai-Li. He could come back at any time,' she urged.

Mai-Li peeled herself reluctantly from the floor and looked around the room.

'There's a broom in the kitchen, I'll get that,' said Rosie. 'And maybe I can find a knife that's not totally blunt. What about something glass that we can break over his head?'

Martha rushed around near her, turning the flat upside down in search of anything they could use. Rosie couldn't help noticing there was less urgency coming from Mai-Li who just seemed to be wandering aimlessly around as if in a trance. Rosie ignored her and busied herself with Martha, where the positivity was strong and reassuring.

Before long, Martha and Rosie had a collection of semi-offensive weapons crowded beside them as they waited on either side of the door.

'What are we going to do about Jelena?' asked Rosie, nodding towards her worryingly lifeless body lying on the bed.

'We'll have to take her with us of course,' replied Martha, looking at Jelena like she'd only just noticed her there. 'We should be able to carry her between the three of us, I reckon. She looks bad, has something happened to her?'

Rosie nodded and then shook her head. 'Not something you want to hear about right now, believe me.' She shivered as the memory tried to push its way into her mind, but Rosie forced it back, replacing it with thoughts of their new mission.

'You think he'll come tonight? It must be quite late,' said Rosie.

'No idea, but we have to be ready whenever he does. And I think we should turn most of the lights off so he can't see what's coming.'

Mai-Li nodded and obligingly turned them all out except for a small lamp in the bedroom, which illuminated part of the bed left empty by Tihana. Rosie could still see the creases she'd made in the sheets, the imprint of her short time in the world. She was everywhere; in the shoes strewn on the floor, the plate of old toast by her bed, the picture of her family on the windowsill. Rosie had never known anyone that had died before but it was like a picture cut out of a magazine: the image no longer visible but that she existed still evident in the hole that remained.

As Rosie stood waiting by the door, anticipation rapidly alternating between excitement and cold hard fear, Rosie recalled all those weeks ago when she was painting on the clifftop; how she'd longed for a distraction from her boring life. Well, she'd certainly got her wish, and then some. But now she wished more than anything she was back on that clifftop, still blissfully unaware of this terrifying world where life had so little value.

Suddenly there was the sound of a key turning in the lock. Rosie raised her weapon above her head and took a deep breath.

# Chapter 24

Ted was unsure whether his plan would guarantee the safe return of his sister or Martha but he really had no choice. As he stood beside a man he hated more than he could remember hating anything else, waiting for Trig, Blue and Saffron, he filled his mind only with how this was helping his sister, not how he was facilitating the escape of an evil criminal.

Trig had refused to have Gabriel in his house so they had arranged to meet at an old warehouse by the river. Trig often used it for shady deals of his own and called it his Country House Retreat, mostly because there was a boat moored up outside for quick exits should the need arise.

Just as Ted thought he could stand the cold no longer, dawn began to break over the river and his bones almost hissed as they thawed in the sun's warm rays. The old run-down building seemed to thaw too as the light touched it, and suddenly it seemed less foreboding. Ted usually loved a sinister looking building with potential for a rave or a place to vent his mischief, but today it was just another dark place like the one he knew Rosie was in.

Suddenly a car appeared from around the other side of the warehouse and pulled up near the water's edge. Ted felt like he was in a movie and this was some kind of exchange: drugs or weapons or a hostage. Then again, it kind of was, except the things he wanted hadn't been brought to the table, they had been promised to him as soon as he dropped Gabriel at the airport. There was no way of knowing whether Gabriel would keep his promise, but what choice did Ted have? He couldn't go to the police; Gabriel had sworn he would never tell where the girls were if anything happened to him. Ted had even considered persuasion Trig-style but he knew that Gabriel was too tough to crack under threat.

Trig, Saffron and Blue stepped out of the car. Then the other back door opened and Dillon got out. Ted immediately bristled at his intrusion; what did he think he was doing here? He hadn't been around when he was really needed and now he was hiding behind Trig's legs like a nervous child. As they walked over, Dillon caught Ted's eye, his look filled with regret and pity, but Ted wasn't ready to forgive him and immediately looked away, focussing on Trig and the girls as if Dillon wasn't there.

Trig nodded at Ted as they came closer and then stared at Gabriel who had his attention focussed solely on Saffron and Blue. Ted watched Trig position himself between the girls and Gabriel's leer, and, despite the fact that Trig's height made little difference to Gabriel's perspective, his assured presence soon got the giant's attention and Gabriel's eyes flicked to the much smaller man.

'No touching, no looking and no talking, got it?' Trig said firmly. Gabriel grinned and nodded, clearly amused by the small man in front of him. Trig lifted his chin towards Saffron and she set about unpacking her make-up whilst Blue unfolded the chair they had brought. Ted could feel their unease at being in such close proximity to Gabriel knowing what he was capable of, but they kept their eyes down and got on with the job in hand, while Trig stood in front of Gabriel's seated body and made sure his eyes stayed facing forwards and his hands never left his lap.

As Saffron worked her magic on Gabriel's face, Ted could feel Dillon's eyes boring into him, begging for forgiveness. At last Ted could stand it no longer and looked at him. Dillon tried to smile, hoping Ted would mirror him, but Ted merely glared. Dillon flicked his head suggesting they step away to talk but Ted wasn't sure he was ready to, especially as he suspected Dillon would get around him, as was usual when they had a disagreement.

'Anything you want to say you can say in front of them,' said Ted, cringing as he heard how that sounded. Dillon blushed and Ted enjoyed seeing him falter as he tried to find the words.

'I wanted to say sorry for not being around the past few days, it's just that my mum's cousin's little girl turned up...' He paused. '...dead. And I had to help her identify the body and then stay with Mum while she contacted her cousin. It was pretty grim, the little girl's body was barely recognisable.'

Ted heard a snort come from Gabriel and turned to see him swallow a laugh as Trig glared at him. The smile stayed though, lying menacingly across his face and twitching occasionally like an impatient cat's tail.

Ted felt awful for assuming Dillon had deserted him. He should have known that he never would have done that. 'I'm sorry, mate… How's your mum?'

'Not great. It appears the girl had been in London, at least for a while – the police managed to catch some of the men responsible – and Mum feels bad that she didn't look harder for her, make more effort to find her. She blames herself.'

Ted didn't know what to say. That it could have been Rosie was all he could think about.

'Anyway, I want to make up for it now,' Dillon said quietly. 'If that's cool?'

'Sure, thanks,' was all Ted could manage as the guilt choked him into silence.

Ted quickly turned his attention and feelings of anger towards Gabriel, but got the shock of his life when he saw that sitting in his place was someone who looked nothing like the man at all. This one was at least twenty years older, had grey hair and glasses. No matter how hard Ted looked he could not see Gabriel anymore.

'Wow, Saffron, that's amazing,' Ted said in awe, despite the hatred for what lay underneath the disguise.

Saffron blushed.

Gabriel lifted his arm tentatively in the air.

'What is it?' snarled Trig.

'Can I see?' asked Gabriel in a mock childlike voice.

Trig nodded at Saffron and she produced a hand mirror. Gabriel took it from her, his gaze lingering on the girl longer than Trig liked, so Trig quickly snatched the mirror from the giant's hand and held it up for him, blocking his view of Saffron.

Gabriel nodded, clearly impressed as he studied his new face in the mirror.

'Not bad. You should come and work for me, little girl,' he said with a grin that Ted was surprised wasn't the excuse Trig needed to wipe the smile off his face. But he stayed calm, presumably for Rosie's sake. 'And what about the passport?'

Blue took her phone out of her pocket and took several pictures of Gabriel's new look. Ted could see her face set in a rigid grimace as she fought to contain her hatred of the subject she was photographing. Ted realised how hard it must be for both girls knowing what Gabriel had done and what he was capable of, and yet having to be in such close proximity.

Whilst Saffron packed away her make-up, Ted watched in awe as Blue pulled out what looked like a tiny printer, attached it to her phone, and printed out the picture, which she then stuck into Gabriel's new passport.

'I'll take him to the airport if you want,' said Trig, not taking his eyes from Gabriel.

'No,' said Gabriel, sternly. 'That wasn't the arrangement. Ted will take me. And only when I'm at the airport and have bought my ticket will I tell him, and only him, where one of the girls are.'

'Why not both?' said Ted desperately; he couldn't only save one, not when the other had helped him so much.

'One was the deal.'

'Dill and I will go to Streatham and wait for a phone call from you, Ted,' said Trig, 'and then go straight to the address he tells you. Here, you can take my car,' he said, tossing the keys at Ted and winking. 'We can pick up Blue's car and take that.'

Did Trig have a plan? wondered Ted. He would just have to trust that he did.

'Remember,' hissed Trig in Gabriel's ear, 'we know what you really look like, and the new name that's in your passport. If you cross us you will be hunted down like the rabid dog that you are and shot. Got it?'

Gabriel grinned. 'Yeah, yeah, I know what a fearsome dude you are. I won't do anything naughty, I promise.' He chuckled. 'Not much movement inside this stuff, is there?' he said, pressing his cheek.

Blue emerged from the car, passport in hand. She gave it to Trig who nodded his appreciation and then handed it to Gabriel who studied it closely before complimenting its authenticity and standing up to leave. 'Well, this has been fun but I've got a plane to catch. Ted?'

Ted hugged Blue and Saffron gratefully and then thanked Trig and Dillon.

'See you soon.' Dillon smiled. 'We'll be waiting by the phone.'

Ted got into the driver's seat and started the engine whilst Gabriel's new identity slid into the passenger seat. Ted hadn't had much driving practise since passing his test but his mind was so focussed on getting to the airport and getting Rosie back that it didn't seem to matter as he sped off, keen to get the whole thing over with.

Gabriel was silent for a long time, which Ted was relieved about. He couldn't imagine anything they could comfortably talk about. Ted just wanted to get him to the airport and then get as far away from him as was physically possible. Then Gabriel broke the silence.

'Which one are you going to choose?' he asked, and Ted could hear the smile in his voice.

'What's to stop me taking both once you're gone?'

Gabriel chuckled. 'Griff.'

'He didn't look like too much of a challenge,' dared Ted, remembering the cowering creature and his weirdness.

'Don't be fooled by him, he's more dangerous than you think.'

'Because he doesn't know what he's doing?' guessed Ted.

'Because he'll do whatever he's told no matter what that is.'

'And what have you told him to do?'

Gabriel laughed again and Ted wanted to slam the car into a wall just to wipe the smirk off.

'Nothing until he gets my message.'

'And then?'

'One for you, one for me.'

'I've done everything you asked!' Ted's voice began to rise. 'Just let them both go!'

'Now why would I do that? Those girls are worth a lot to me.'

'They're worth more to me!' said Ted desperately. 'I'll do whatever you want, take me instead,' he said, tears blurring the road.

'Oh come on, Teddy, you were doing so well, don't fall apart on me now,' he sneered.

'Fuck you,' replied Ted through gritted teeth, forcing himself to focus on the traffic ahead of him which was now speeding up as two lanes became three. They were only a few minutes from the airport and he hadn't managed to convince Gabriel to free both the girls. His only hope was that Trig really did have a plan.

They found a short-stay car park and Ted followed Gabriel to departures. Gabriel wouldn't let him see the destination of his flight, so Ted stood back, his eyes never leaving the giant as he bought his ticket.

Eventually Gabriel walked back towards Ted. 'Well, you've stuck admirably to your side of the deal so I guess it's my turn. The address is 8 Church Road, and they're in one of the first-floor flats. Griff will only give them one so make sure it's the right one.' He smiled before turning and heading for the departure gates. Ted quickly pulled out his phone and called Dillon, telling him to do whatever it took to get both the girls.

Hanging up, he stood motionless in the sea of people hurrying past, no longer feeling part of the world he once knew. There were at least eight flights that were currently boarding and he had no idea which one was Gabriel's.

His phone rang – it was Dillon.

'They're not here!' he shouted. 'Don't let him go!'

Ted's heart leapt to the back of his throat. 'What do you mean they're not there, they have to be,' he yelled.

'Someone was here but not anymore, and…' Dillon paused.

'And what, Dillon?' said Ted desperately.

'And there's blood on the floor.'

# Chapter 25

The speed and force with which Rosie brought down her weapon on the man's head surprised even her. And immediately after her blow had struck, Martha was there to echo it. But as the body slumped onto the floor, still conscious, Rosie suddenly saw who it was.

'Griff!'

But Martha wasn't waiting for a response, quickly following her first strike with another to his back, her broom handle shattering as it made impact. Without pausing, she turned to reach for something else, determination set heavy in her brow. Griff was not easily broken though, and he began to crawl across the room towards Mai-Li's cowering body. He grabbed her foot and she screamed, kicking at him with the other. Then, before any of them knew what was happening, Griff had pulled Mai-Li's foot with all his strength and dragged her down next to him.

A knife shone menacingly at her throat. Martha froze, mid-strike.

'Put. That. Down,' hissed Griff, clutching Mai-Li's trembling body to him. Rosie could see he'd already drawn blood so she stepped back, dropping her weapon. Martha did the same.

Griff struggled to sit up, wincing in pain. He pulled Mai-Li up beside him and then sat glaring at Martha and Rosie, obviously trying to decide what his next move should be.

Martha looked defiant, but Rosie didn't have the same confidence and was suddenly gripped with the terrible realisation that yet again she had made things worse for everyone.

Griff held Mai-Li close as he stood, the knife pressing into her neck so hard it was creating a pocket of blood that was dripping slowly onto the floor. Rosie realised now why Mai-Li was so reluctant to go along with their plan; she had probably been here before, more than once, and the disappointment of a failed escape was turning out to be worse than not trying at all.

Griff ordered Martha and Rosie to sit on the bed beside Jelena. Rosie wondered how much of this Jelena was even aware of; her face showing no reaction.

'You shouldn't have done that,' he said, looking at Rosie.

'We just want to go home,' Rosie whispered, now seeing the man that Mai-Li had been talking about in the steady hand that held the knife to her neck. How had she been so blind?

'Home?' Griff sneered. 'You're never going home.'

Rosie gulped. She could feel Martha pulsating with anger next to her and was afraid of what she might do or say.

'We're leaving. Now!' shouted Griff.

Rosie jumped. 'Where are we going?'

'Far away from here, so far that no one will find you,' he snarled.

Rosie felt sick, did he mean to another country?

'You're not taking me anywhere,' said Martha defiantly.

'Always the same, the new ones, until they are tamed, isn't that right, Mai-Li?' said Griff, licking her face.

Mai-Li tried to pull away but the knife bit into her neck and she squeaked in pain.

Like a mother reacting to her baby's cry, so Jelena lifted her head slowly from the bed, her eyes wild as she glared at Griff. Rosie and Martha stood up as she swung her legs off the bed and screamed a scream so terrifying and desperate that Rosie felt the vibrations inside her very soul. Jelena launched herself at a surprised Griff; biting and scratching at his face and anything she could get hold of. He plunged the knife into her repeatedly but she didn't seem to feel it in her adrenalin-fuelled fury.

Martha sprang forward and smashed his hand away with a chair leg, a roar from Griff echoing the sound of shattering bone. He dropped the knife, as well as Mai-Li, and clutched his arm, just as Rosie, mustering all her strength and courage as well as memories of the pain and suffering she and all the other girls had been put through, placed the final blow straight to his face with the back of a chair. Blood spurted from his nose; then there was silence.

They all waited, holding their breath, expecting him to move, but his body lay motionless. Martha prodded him, but nothing. Rosie was shaking as she dropped her weapon and went to hug Mai-Li. Martha joined them and the three of them trembled in a heap.

Martha was the first to pull away. 'We've gotta go!' she said urgently. 'We don't know how long it will be before someone else turns up.'

Rosie leaped to her feet and pulled at Mai-Li's arm. She didn't budge.

'Come on,' she said, heading for the door. 'We may not have much time!'

Mai-Li shook her head.

Rosie looked down at Griff's body next to Mai-Li's feet. 'I can move him if you're afraid to go past,' she said, pulling at one of Griff's feet and dragging him a little way away from Mai-Li.

But Mai-Li still shook her head.

Martha was busy trying to get a hold on Jelena's now limp body to lift her off the floor. She was bleeding from several places and flitting in and out of consciousness. Rosie ran to grab the other side.

'Come on, Mai-Li, we need help with Jelena!' shouted Rosie, fear filling her chest as the time ticked on.

But Mai-Li wouldn't move, she just sat shaking her head, her knees tucked up under her chin. Rosie and Martha half lifted, half dragged Jelena's body out of the door, but as Rosie looked back Mai-Li was still sitting in the same place, her eyes wide with fear, her body rocking back and forth.

Rosie dropped her side of Jelena and went back into the room.

'Please, Mai-Li, we have to go. Don't be afraid, I won't let anything happen to you.'

'I can't,' whispered Mai-Li.

And as Rosie watched her little body shivering in the corner she realised that Mai-Li couldn't bring herself to leave this room any more than that bird Captain could leave its cage.

Rosie bent down and hugged her; tears pouring silently down her face.

'I'll come back for you, I promise.'

Mai-Li just looked at her and nodded slowly. Rosie saw no hope in her eyes; all the fight had gone. She hugged her one last time and leapt up to help Martha carry Jelena down the stairs and out into the daylight.

# Epilogue

Rosie pressed her face against the train window, her eyes flickering as she tried not to miss anything. Everything had taken on a whole different hue, brighter, more beautiful than she remembered. The grass so green, the sky so blue, it was a picture-book world where the colours never faded and the story told of rabbits and rainbows and pots of gold.

Suddenly the colour and light disappeared, and only her face was visible as darkness engulfed the speeding train as it rattled through a tunnel. Not for the first time was she surprised by the look in the eyes of the person staring back; darker than she remembered and disappointed, as if something hadn't happened the way it should and now they couldn't forget and go back.

She jumped as light tore through the train again and her face vanished. She felt a reassuring hand on her leg and turned to smile at Ted. He had hardly left her side since she had escaped nearly two months ago, his eyes ever watchful, protective, terrified of letting her out of his sight again. The regret and guilt he felt oozed out of him with every expression, every movement, every look he gave Rosie.

Rosie in comparison was dealing with it all in a much more positive way. She regularly checked in on Baduwa and Jelena, who were coincidently together at the same girls' home. Baduwa had taken Jelena under her wing and was slowly repairing her damaged body and soul with her positivity and bright, colourful spirit, which at last had found its much-needed sanctuary. It made Rosie laugh to see Jelena made-up and preened to within an inch of her life; decorated with lipstick and hair clips, her sad empty eyes highlighted with colourful eyeshadow. Jelena couldn't have helped smiling when looking at herself in the mirror, even if it was because a clown was smiling back.

Both girls had been allowed to stay in the country, although Jelena wanted to return to Norway one day to see her family. Baduwa was determined to make a life for herself in England; to have the job and house she had been promised all those months ago, and to save enough money to get her mother and sisters out of Nigeria. Baduwa had never mentioned Utibe on any of the occasions Rosie visited, and Rosie couldn't bring herself to think about it, so Utibe's memory became the occasional flash that was quickly batted away before it forced itself uninvited into their conscience.

'You want a drink?' Ted's voice broke into Rosie's thoughts.

Rosie nodded, insisting she'd like to come with him, stretch her legs.

The train was busy, and as she walked down the aisle, eyes lifted and heads turned in her direction, followed by the occasional whisper as if her movement had stirred wind in the trees. Rosie felt immediately self-conscious because she wasn't sure if it was that they were just curious about who was passing or that they recognised her; after all, her story had been in all the newspapers and on the news, as Martha had promised. And, despite her being a minor, she had insisted on telling her story personally; Martha had said the only way to get people to really care was if they actually got to know her as a person. Otherwise she was just another faceless statistic. Rosie's mum and dad hadn't been happy about it, of course – they just wanted to forget about the whole nightmare and get on with their lives – but Rosie had told them that she needed a better reason for why it had happened to her other than she was just in the wrong place at the wrong time. And if it was to save others from the same fate then she could accept that as her lot, and maybe one day come to terms with it and move on. They understood, reassuring Rosie they wanted only the best for her and that she should do exactly what she needed to do to help her get through it.

Rosie smiled at the thought of her parents. It had been the most amazing feeling when she'd seen them for the first time after so long. It was at that moment she had known it was all finally over. It hadn't been the person in the car that slammed on the brakes as the three girls staggered out into the road screaming, or the paramedics as they were taken to the hospital. It had been seeing her mum and dad when they walked into her hospital room that finally made all the fear and sadness fall away. It was like coming home.

And then suddenly Ted was there, hugging all of them, and Rosie was laughing and crying, and trying to breathe as Ted held her so tightly and cried into her hair. And she squeezed him back, like she never wanted to let go, and thanked him over and over for all he'd done.

And there had never been a time that Rosie could remember feeling so happy and so safe, and so completely in love with her family, who hadn't given up on her even after everything she had put them through in the past. It was the moment she had dreamed about for so long and she never wanted it to end.

Rosie and Ted walked into the buffet carriage, the smell of bacon hitting their noses. A few people were eating and drinking, some turning to look as they entered. While they waited to be served, a woman walked up to Rosie, her eyes filled with the same pity that Rosie now knew so well. 'I have a daughter who's your age. Since I heard your story I have been terrified that the same thing may happen to her. There seems to be no discrimination in the traffickers' selection, anyone can be a victim.'

Rosie nodded, a little taken aback. This had happened a few times to her already and each time it was so surreal, like they were talking to someone else.

The woman gripped Rosie's hand and smiled. 'Seems some of the stories have a happy ending though. Stay safe.'

As the woman walked away Rosie was aware that everyone had stopped what they were doing and were staring. She pulled Ted by the arm and dragged him out of the carriage, back to their seats where she resumed her absorption in what was going on outside the window.

'Do you want to stay here while I get the drinks?' asked Ted

Rosie nodded without taking her eyes off the passing fields and houses.

***

Ted made his way back down the train. He still marvelled at the power of the press. Trafficking had gone from being a dirty little secret whispered between nations to a full-blown initiative embraced by everyone, all because it had happened to a white British girl and was now too close to home to be ignored. The sleeping giants that were the continents had been awoken from their slumber by a fourteen-year-old girl's story, and now they were sending ripples of action through the countries in an attempt to stamp human trafficking out.

Not for the first time, Ted thought of Martha and how she had played such a huge part in saving Rosie. Her story had been in every newspaper and on every news programme across the world. You could almost hear people stirring and saying to each other, I had no idea this was going on, did you? Why did no one tell us? Why has no one done anything about this already? It should never have been allowed to go on for so long!

Ted ordered drinks for them, his eyes wandering around the room as he waited. He had fears of his own; fears that Griff was still out there somewhere. Gabriel too. And then there was Silas. When the police had gone back to the house, at Rosie's request to find Mai-Li, the place was deserted. There was no sign of Griff's body, nor of Mai-Li, and the rooms downstairs were all empty too. Rosie had been distraught; she had blamed herself for not dragging Mai-Li out of there when she'd had the chance. She had been so desperate to get away it hadn't crossed her mind that Mai-Li may not be there when someone came back a few hours later.

Ted collected the drinks and walked back to Rosie. Her breath had misted up the window and she was drawing faces with her finger. She turned and smiled when she felt him sit down.

Ted's phone rang. 'Hi Martha,' he said, grinning at Rosie. 'Yeah, we're fine. How are you? Really? That's great news! Yup. Yeah, we're still on for tomorrow, we're on our way up to London now. Yes, the house is great, nowhere near the sea and close enough to London for us to visit regularly. Yeah, I miss you too. See you tomorrow then.'

'That was quick,' said Rosie.

'She was rushing to a press conference; there's been a huge police raid on a suspected trafficker's house in Manchester. It's the epicentre of a massive trafficking ring and they've busted loads of the people responsible, and rescued hundreds of women and children,' he said excitedly.

Rosie beamed. She had never seen her brother so mushy over a girl. She could feel his nervousness at seeing her the next day, and it made her want to giggle.

'She was just ringing to check we were still OK to do the interview tomorrow. You are, aren't you?'

Rosie nodded. She hated being at the centre of all this attention; she wished in a way that she could go back to her life of blissful ignorance, bury her head in the sand and pretend none of it was happening. But for some reason she had been through all that horror so the world would sit up and take notice, and she thought that knowing she was helping others was, in turn, probably helping her to deal with everything that had happened rather than burying it deep where it would fester like an untreated wound.

'The next station is London Waterloo where this train will terminate,' came the voice over the intercom.

Rosie and Ted gathered their bags. They were staying at their uncle's house whilst in town, but Rosie had insisted on visiting Lo at the boys' home on their way, as she tried to do each time she was in London. Rosie was helping Lo with his English. The authorities had been unable to track down his family so he couldn't go home, and Rosie wanted him to have the best chance of finding someone to adopt him. He was still very introverted and the staff at the home said he often woke screaming in the night, but that during the day he was gradually coming out of his shell and playing with the other boys. He was always really pleased to see Rosie, a grin spreading across his face every time she entered the room. Helping him was her small way of giving back some of what had been taken away. And he gave her purpose too; he was the cement that was gradually filling in the huge hole left by everything that had happened.

The taxi arrived at the boys' home, and Ted and Rosie grabbed their bags and walked up to the door. As they heard the bell echo throughout the inside of the huge building, Rosie pictured the happy grin that would welcome her, the face that gave her hope for the future. But when the door eventually swung open, it was Andrew, the manager of the boys' home, that greeted them, not Lo, and Rosie sensed there was something wrong. His expression was troubled as he led them through the corridors to his office, gesturing towards the two seats on the other side of his desk and folding his hands under his chin as he looked at them both with sorrow in his eyes.

'Lo has gone,' he said quietly. 'He went missing yesterday and no one has seen him since.'

Rosie leapt from her chair and rushed out into the corridor. She ran through the halls, opening all the doors to startled eyes beyond. She could hear Ted behind her calling her name, begging her to stop.

'Lo!' she shouted. 'Where are you, Lo? It's Rosie, I've come to take you away from this awful place.'

The squeak from her shoes on the wooden floors as she searched each room echoed her frenzied cries. Why was he not here?

'Lo, darling, please come out,' she called again.

Finally Ted caught up to her and held her tight in his arms as she thrashed around, trying to pull out of his grip.

'He's gone,' Ted whispered into her hair over and over again.

Rosie eventually submitted and, sobbing, allowed herself to be half carried back to Andrew's office. She was aware of frightened eyes on her as she passed the rooms she'd searched, and all she could say was sorry.

Ted placed her gently back in the chair, where she sat, head down, tears dripping silently from her eyes.

'Do you have any idea where he might have gone?' asked Ted, sternly. 'Surely this shouldn't happen.'

Andrew shook his head. 'It shouldn't happen, but it does. We just don't have the staff to watch every child twenty-four-seven. Some run away and others are taken back by the very people we saved them from in the first place. And until we get more funding I'm afraid it will continue to happen. I'm so sorry.'

Rosie looked up at Andrew, his edges blurred. 'But Lo wouldn't have run away...' she whispered.

Andrew shook his head again. 'No... no, he wouldn't have run away...'

'So that means...' Rosie couldn't say the words, her voice muted by a terrifying realisation, one that sucked the breath from her: Lo was back in that world, alone and unloved. A tiny ghost in a giant House of Horrors.

# Note from the Author

Although all the characters in this book are fictional, child trafficking is most definitely not. Each one of the characters plays a role to give you an idea of the kind of horror that trafficking can bring, whether to a middle-class white girl with a family that cares about her, or a poor Nigerian girl whose family sold her for a few pennies to feed themselves. Many of the characters were developed from real-life stories I read when doing my research; the age groups, the nationalities – there is no discrimination in the world of trafficking; anyone and everyone is a potential victim for anything from prostitution to slave labour.

When I first heard about child trafficking I was shocked that such exploitation of innocent human lives was allowed to go on. I was sure slavery had been abolished years ago, and yet here we still are, probably sitting not too far from someone who is doing something against their will at the hands of a much more evil and manipulative other.

Much like Ted did on the Tube, I found myself looking around more at people and trying to guess which, if any, might have some child locked away at home cleaning the floors, or out making money for them like Rosie and the other girls were forced to do. Of course it's impossible to tell, mostly because the diversity of culture, especially in our cities, means that people can be trafficked around relatively freely without alerting suspicion, which also makes it a very hard crime to keep track of and stop.

As in Lo's case, it is very common for children to be re-trafficked. Even if the authorities manage to rescue the children and place them in care, they are often kidnapped again within a few months.

I have listed a few statistics and websites below (correct at the time of printing), where you can find out more information if you would like to get involved with helping children like Lo, Baduwa, Utibe, Mai-Li, Jelena, Tihana, and of course, Rosie.


Human trafficking is the second largest source of illegal income worldwide, exceeded only by drugs. (belser, 2005)


At least 12.3 million people are victims of forced labour worldwide. Of these, 2.4 million are as a result of human trafficking.
(*A global alliance against forced labour*, International Labour Organisation, 2005)


1.2 million children are trafficked every year. (Estimate by UNICEF)


People trafficking is the fastest growing means by which people are enslaved, the fastest growing international crime, and one of the largest sources of income for organised crime. (The UN Office on Drugs and Crime)

Types of recruitment include abduction, false agreement with parents, sold by parents, runaways, travel with family, orphans sold from street or institutions.

(http://www.stopthetraffik.org/humantrafficking/problem.aspx)

Human trafficking is a 'low risk, high profit' crime, with annual profits of $32 billion.

(http://www.crin.org/docs/ChildSlaveryBrieffinal.pdf Save the Children UK.)

In 2006 there were only 5,808 prosecutions and 3,160 convictions throughout the world. This means that for every 800 people trafficked, only one person was convicted. (US State Department, *Trafficking in Persons Report*, 2007, p.36)

ECPAT UK stands for End Child Prostitution, Child Pornography and the Trafficking of Children for Sexual Purposes. They are a leading children's rights organisation campaigning against the commercial and sexual exploitation of children in the UK and on its international aspects. www.ecpat.org.uk

Stop the Traffik is a global movement of individuals, communities and organisations fighting to prevent human trafficking around the world. www.stopthetraffik.org

I refer quite a bit to Nigeria, particularly when mentioning the child witches. This part was also taken from true accounts

I'd read about in my research. Helping these children is a charity called Save Child Africa, they can be found here: www.safechildafrica.org